HOW TO SETUP
BUSINESS
IN USA
BASIC GUIDE

Keshav lal CPA NJ USA

BlueRose ONE
Stories Matter

First Published in April 2023

ISBN: 978-93-5704-545-2

E-ISBN: 978-93-5741-590-3

BLUEROSE PUBLISHERS

www.BlueRoseONE.com

info@bluerosepublishers.com

+91 8882 898 898

Cover Design:

Yash

Typographic Design:

Tanya Raj Upadhyay

Distributed by: BlueRose, Amazon, Flipkart

Disclaimer

This book has been written as a manual for general knowledge and in layman language, and may not have valid and UpToDate information. Book is not design as a substitute of legal and professional advice. Author strongly recommends to seek legal and professional advice in your situation in any matter of your interest or explore for valid and UpToDate information.

Thanks.

With Best Wishes: Keshav Lal.

Acknowledgements

I am thankful to my friends and students for their ever best wishes:

Mr. Gary S. Pasricha

Mr. Jaswant S. Bal

Mr. Kuljit S. Pelia

Mr. Manjit Singh

Mr. Nirmal P. Chopra

Mr. Ravi R. Boodhanuru

Mr. Rajiv Vaish

And all other friends.

I want to thank all my family members who had been ever supporting in this project.

Thanks to everyone in BlueRose Publication. Special thanks to Ms. Shirley, Publication Manager. I had an excellent experience working with all members of publication team for their special support and care to a new author.

How to Set up Business in USA

This book is a masterpiece for the readers who want to explore business settlement in USA. This book is not an official guide or legal reference, and will not cover legal procedures or legal codes, or rules and regulations, rather has been written based on general experiences, information and practices. This book is written simply by gathering general information that may not support any legal regulation, therefore, any legal solution and guidance is out of scope of this book, for which one may have to consult accounting, tax and legal consultants or relevant State and Federal Agencies.

Other, the purpose of the book is to give its readers a general and very basic idea about the business setting process in USA, and each component will need further exploration and suitable criteria. Setting business in USA is a vast matter, the total coverage will be beyond the scope of this book. Contents in the book are not gathered from legal codes, rather based on day-to-day experiences and general information available to author.

Because the book contains general information which may or may not be of any use in your situation, the authors do not take any responsibility for accuracy and validity of any information contained in the book.

Hope keeping in view all these limitations, the book will be of great interest and will provide valuable directions and knowledge to the business community of the world.

About the Book

This book is being authored by Keshav Lal CPA-NJ-USA. The purpose of this book is to discuss about USA and initial settlement steps in a very simple and layman's language just to have some basic understanding on settling in the USA. The most part of my own experience and other of similar cases. I hope the discussion will be better for new immigrants with the information of some of important essentials. Book has limit to cover all of each and every and every aspect of life, and also include the detailed discussion on each topic. But still author believe the topics discussed in the book will be helpful in several alerts.

The topics of this book are from the thought process of my long experience and knowledge and will not support any legal content. Actually, each topic and term has vast and special rules, how they should be treated, and a complete discussion is out of the scope of this book.

This book is good only to get some knowledge in one place relating to settling in USA, though has escaped several topics beyond my capacity and knowledge.

I am a professional as CPA but not an Author, therefore, readers may encounter with various flaws in slangs and language. I will be very sorry for these flaws but request to take all topics in the same sense for which those are written for. Most of the part is written in American spellings, and you may find some variation in nouns as used in other countries.

Books is not a substitute of legal advice and I suggest consulting your professionals from time to time for your various needs, specially with legal matter such as immigration, and author will not take any responsibility for any incorrect aspect of the contents in this book. Readers are highly suggested to consult their professionals or explore for detailed, correct, and UpToDate information.

Some Terms Used in The Book:

Employer: All kind of employer such as sole proprietor, LLC, Corporations

Tax   USA Tax or State Tax

State   Among USA States

He-Him-His   All Individuals:

IRS   Internal Revenue Service: USA Federal Tax Agency

NJ   New Jersey: One of the USA State

State   USA State

Why information about New Jersey only:Because all my experience is in New Jersey, and this book is written based on my knowledge and not on research.

Why Published from India: I chose an Indian publication house, because I am an Indian born US Citizen. India is a vast and fast-growing Country. Therefore, I thought it better to launch my book in India, though the book is good for every Country.

About the Author

This valuable manual has been authored by Mr. Keshav Lal, M Com, MA- Eco, MBA, and CPA. Mr. Lal is a former professor in Commerce and Business Administration from Punjab State College affiliated with Punjabi University Patiala.

Mr. Lal is an Indian born US Citizen, and possesses four masters' degrees:

Masters' in Commerce

Masters' in Economics

Masters' in History

Masters' in Philosophy (Business Administration).

Mr. Lal is a Certified Public Accountant in USA for the 20 years and has his own practice.

Mr. Lal is highly educated and talented person who possesses diversified experiences and knowledge. His areas of expertise are:

- International Accounting and Taxation
- International Business Setting and consulting.
- Accounting, Financial Statements, Financial Analysis and Processing Financial information & data.
- Taxation at USA level and at international level.
- Taxation: Income Tax, Payroll Taxes, Sales Tax & Corporate (Business) Taxes-All States and Federal Taxes.
- Payroll, Payroll Returns & Payroll Taxes (Complete Cycle and Consulting).
- Legal Functions (Accounting & Taxation) Business Law, Labor Laws, Immigration Process relating with Salary and Wage, fringe benefits, hiring process, termination process, able to

understand and handle all disputes with employees', vendors' & clients through appropriate law firms and agencies.

- HR Functions (Accounting & Taxation) Handling employment issues, developing hiring policies, developing handbooks, salary structure, benefits structure, establishing cost-production relation etc.
- Advance & complex accounting, costing & budgeting and budgetary control.
- Setting supervision systems, setting self-supervisory internal control, setting responsibility centers, establishing authority-responsibility centers, developing managerial goals, and developing supervisory control systems.
- Conducting audit functions-internal audit: Developing & implementing Audit Techniques And comply with Internal Auditing Rules-Sarbanes-Oxley.

It took a long way to gather the information by using own experience and knowledge, before Mr. Lal is able to put together the whole package. Mr. Lal does expect various flaws and shortcomings in the manuals, but he hopes keeping in view several limitations for the project, readers will escape all such attentions and will excuse keeping in view his best efforts as he has taken.

Keshav Lal

Table of Contents

About America

There are huge number of people who will be dreaming for America and want to settle in America, but a smaller number of people really know about America. The most people are attracted to dollar's value and beauty of the country. Other group is focusing for job or business opportunities and has heard lot of things about America, and further people have just a big craze to settle abroad.

There are lots about America, which cannot be covered in the chapter. But the author will try to include certain basic information about America that may be of your interest and value to you.

America is huge country well known as "Land of Opportunities".

Geography

World has been naturally divided into five continents:

1) Asia
2) America
3) Africa
4) Europe
5) Australia

America is one of these five continents. America continent is in between two giant oceans. On its east side is "Atlantic Ocean" and west side is "Pacific Oceans". The whole continent is further divided in three zones viz: North America, Central America and South America. America Continent is a group of about 50 countries and USA is one of them.

Central America is very thin and, therefore, Atlantic Ocean and Pacific Ocean are joined together through man made canal known as "Panama Canal".

America is not a country but a full continent.

USA, which is well known, as "America", is one of the countries located in America continent. USA is located in North America. Other major country in North America is Canada. Because USA is the most popular or being top most country in America continent, name "America" stand for USA in common language.

Official Name:	United States of America
Short Name	United States or "the States"
Abbreviated	USA
Short Abbreviated	US
Currency Code	USD (US Dollar)
Currency Symbol	US$ (International)
	$ (Local)
Capital	Washington DC.

Brief History

Italian born Christopher Columbus, with the support of Isabella I, Queen of Spain has found America during his few ventures between 1492-1506. Since then, America became major settlement attraction by major European Countries, such as Great Britain, Spain & France. Eventually the Britain had strong hold in the continent, and was able to establish 13 colonies. With passage of time, these colonies organized themselves and declared independence from Britain in 1776 and organized into a Federation known as "United States of America". Originally, they were 13 colonies, but the federation expanded into 50 States by further joining more States into the federation, and by acquiring territories in major deals from other countries.

In March 1803: The federation bought territory known as "Louisiana Territory" and "New Orleans" from Napoleon Bonaparte of France. Before Napoleon Bonaparte had acquired these territories from Spain in a secrete treaty in October 1800 under a peace settlement with Spain.

But then Napoleon Bonaparte realized that developing these territories would be more trouble than the worth.

He wanted to concentrate on his European Empire where future wars were expected and he needed the money.

Due to his troubles in Civil War in Haiti he lost the interest in these territories.

He was fearing that these territories otherwise could be annexed by any enemy country in any war.

With all these factors he sold the Louisianan Territory to the USA-federation, merely for low price as three cent per acre, by keeping in mind this deal will improve his relation with USA which will help him and sale money in wars against British.

During American-Mexican War (1845-1848) Mexico signed peace treaty on February 2, 1848. According to the treaty, Mexico ceded to the United States nearly all the territory now included in the States of New Mexico, Utah, Nevada, Arizona, California, Texas, and western Colorado for $15 million.

In March 1867: USA purchase Alaska from Russia for $7.2M at 2cent per acre.

In this way United States expanded its territories and became a huge country of 50 States.

The so-called Federation (USA) is a union of 50 countries. They are called "States", but they are independent countries. Each "State" has its own constitution, flag, rules and regulation, education system, business policies etc., but they are one for other purposes such as military, currency, foreign Policy and for other matters of common interest. We will talk about State structure later.

Area

USA is a huge country in area. Its total area is 9,631,418 sq. kms and land area is 9,161,923 sq. kms. According to comparative study, USA is three times bigger than India, about half of Russia, about half of south America, slightly larger than China, about two and half times of western Europe. USA is world's third largest country area wise being Russia at number one and Canada at number two.

Population

Total population of USA is estimate 331M (About 33 Crores (2020)) Canada 38M (about 4 crores) UK 67M (about 7 crores) India 1380M (About 138 crores). For comparative purposes it is the third populated country, being China at number one, and India at number two. From this comparison do not assess USA as a populated country. Keeping in view the total area USA is not a highly populated country.

Population per Sq Mile 94

Population Growth	0.4 % (2020)		
Birth Rate	12/1000 Population		
Death Rate	8.9/1000 Population		
Immigration Rate	2.820/1000 Population		
Life Expectancy Rate	78.79 Years over all		
	78.8 Years-Male		
	81.4 Years-Female		
Ethnic Groups	White	75.8	%
	Black	13.6	%
	Asian	6.1	%
	Other	4.5	%
Religion	Protestant	52	%

Roman Catholic	24	%
Mormon	2	%
Muslim	1	%
Jewish	1	%
Other	19	%

Language   English

Spanish

(In private life people speak their native language as well. It is told about 150 languages are spoken in private life.)

States

Name	Abbreviation	Area	Population approximately	Nickname
ALABAMA	AL	52,423 SqM	5.05M	YELLOW HAMMER STATE
ALASKA	AK	663,267 SqM	0.7M	THE LAST FRONTIER
ARIZONA	AZ	113,998 SqM	7.2M	THE Grand Canyon STATE
ARKANSAS	AR	53,182 SqM	3.0m	THE NATURAL STATE
CALIFORNIA	CA	163,707 SqM	39.8M	GOLDEN STATE
COLORADO	CO	104,100 SqM	5.8M	COLORFUL COLORADO
CONNECTICUT	CT	5,544 SqM	3.6M	CONSTITUTION STATE
DELAWARE	DE	2,489 SqM	1.0M	FIRST STATE/DIAMOND STATE
FLORIDA	FL	65,758 SqM	21.8M	SUNSHINE STATE
GEORGIA	GA	59,425 SqM	10.8M	PEACH STATE
HAWAII	HI	10,932 SqM	1.5M	ALOHA STATE
IDAHO	ID	83,574	1.8M	GEM STATE

		SqM		
ILLINOIS	IL	57,918 SqM	12.8M	PRAIRIE STATE
INDIANA	IN	36,420 SqM	6.8M	THE HOOSIER STATE
IOWA	IA	56,276 SqM	3.2M	THE HAWKEYE STATE
KANSAS	KS	82,282 SqM	2.9M	SUNFLOWER STATE
KENTUCKY	KT	40,411 SqM	4.5M	BLUEGRASS STATE
LOUISIANA	LA	51,843 SqM	4.6M	PELICAN STATE
MAINE	ME	35,387 SqM	1.4M	PINE TREE STATE
MARYLAND	MD	12,407 SqM	6.2M	OLD LINE STATE
MASSACHUSETTS	MA	10,555 SqM	7.0M	BAY STATE
MICHIGAN	MI	96,810 SqM	10.0M	WOLVERINE STATE
MINNESOTA	MN	86,943 SqM	5.7M	NORTH STARE STATE
MISSISSIPPI	MS	48,434 SqM	2.9M	MANNOLIA STATE
MISSOURI	MO	69,709 SqM	6.2M	SHOW ME STATE
MONTANA	MT	147,046 SqM	1.1M	TREASURE STATE
NEBRASKA	NE	77,358 SqM	1.9M	CORNHUSKER STATE
NEVADA	NV	110,567 SqM	3.1M	THE SILVER STATE
NEW HAMPSHIRE	NH	9,351 SqM	1.4M	GRANITE STATE
NEW JERSEY	NJ	8,722 SqM	9.3M	GARDEN STATE
NEW MEXICO	NM	121,593 SqM	2.1M	LAND OF ENCHANTMENT
NEW YORK	NY	54,475 SqM	20.3M	EMPIRE STATE
NORTH CAROLINA	NC	53,821 SqM	10.5M	TAR HEEL STATE

NORTH DAKOTA	ND	70,704 SqM	0.8M	PLEAGE GARDEN STATE
OHIO	OH	44,828 SqM	11.8M	BUCKEYE STATE
OKLAHOMA	OK	69903SQ MI	4.0M	SOONER STATE
OREGON	OR	98,386 SqM	4.2M	BEAVER STATE
PENNSYLVANIA	PA	46,058 SqM	13.0M	KEYSTONE STATE
RHODE ISLAND	RI	1,515 SqM	1.1M	THE OCEAN STATE
SOUTH CAROLINA	SC	32,007 SqM	5.1M	PALMETTO STATE
SOUTH DAKOTA	SD	77,121 SqM	0.9M	MOUNT RUSHMORE STATE
TENNESSEE	TN	42,146 SqM	6.10M	VOLUNTEER STATE
TEXAS	TX	268,601 SqM	29.5M	LONE STAR STATE
UTAH	UT	84,904 SqM	3.3M	THE BECHIVE STATE
VERMONT	VT	9,615 SqM	06M	GREEN MOUNTAIN STATE
VIRGINIA	VA	42,769 SqM	8.6M	OLD DOMINION STATE
WASHINGTON	WA	71,303 SqM	7.8M	THE EVERGREEN STATE
WEST VIRGINIA	WV	24,231 SqM	1.8M	MOUNTAIN STATE
WISCONSIN	WI	65,503 SqM	5.9M	BADGER STATE
WYOMING	WY	97,818 SqM	0.6M	EQUALITY STATE

Note: Area ranks wise, Alaska State is the largest with area of 663,267 Sq. MI, and smallest is Rhode Island with area of 1,545 Sq. MI. The nickname of each State has its own importance and fascination. It is hard to say how and when they were generated, but seems to be associated with political and natural reasons and importance behind them. For example, Keystone State (PA) - Independence was declared from Pennsylvania State, Constitution State- Constitution of USA was written in Connecticut, Evergreen State, because Washington has lot of rain and so on.

States have other peculiar features such as some are good for residence, other for agriculture, some are mixed, some are industrial establishments, some have strong financial institutions establishments, and some are good for trading, international trading and businesses. Similarly, some States are more known as immigrant States such as New Jersey and New York, reason these States have more immigrant population from all over the world. On other counter some states are very cold round the year specially in the part of north America, southern States are hot round the year, western States have lot of rain, central States go for four weathers cycle.

America has immigrants from almost from every country. Immigrants have also arranged TV Channels and Music Channels of their native countries in their native languages.

Dresses

America is full of variety of dresses for men, women and children almost in modern fashion to classical. But main clothing is Blue Jean, T-shirts and Snickers. Blue jean and snickers are commonly worn by men, women of all ages and children. Being a secular country, you have full freedom to maintain your culture, dressing and outlook. On roads and in malls you can easily find several people wearing their classic country dresses and people in their religious and cultural physical appearances.

Shopping Centers & Stores:

America has variety of modes for shopping and buying. Almost in all big cities we have big malls (chain of stores under one roof in a big building) those have variety of stores. There are private stores and Corporation stores mostly called store-chains. Big Corporations own these stores and run them under their own name brand banners. Rates are very competitive. One can buy low priced, mid-priced and high-priced items. All stores and distributors try their best to maintain the quality of the product. Customer service is very important in all businesses that means customer is considered very important. Store managers and all store workers provide all comfort to help the customers. You will not feel bothered by storeowners or store workers in buying and selection. Sizes of such stores are huge and you can walk around a lot and pick up the stuff of your choice. Prices are fixed and tagged. After you buy, and if you do not like later, you can come back and return the items within 30 days with no hassle. Such kind of environment exists in almost all types of stores such as electronic stores, computer stores, office stationary stores, grocery stores and all others. Customer service is important everywhere including theaters, telephone companies, public offices and other service centers. Sales persons and counter cashiers provide services with all smiles and using courtesy language, such as "how I can help you". "you need any help" etc. Using "thanking you" and "you welcome" are very popular slangs being used. During your shopping, you will not feel any pressure or other restraints.

Food

Having outside food is very common here. Because outside food is good, tasty with lot of varieties and comparatively less expensive. One can go and eat in the store, or bring at home (commonly called take out) and can even order on phone and food will be delivered at your home. There are lot of franchise chains of fast-food stores such as Mcdonald, BurgerKing, WhiteCastle, BostonMarket etc. There are other stores/restaurants for specialized food such as Chinese Food, Mexican Food, Italian Food, Indian Restaurant, and South Indian Restaurant etc. There are Diners where one can go and order food of choice. Diners are good place to spend time but little expensive. So, people usually go there for dating, to celebrate birthdays, or on Friday evening etc.

Special Events

Friday Eve: Friday evening is considered the most enjoyable evening. Because people are happy after working for whole week, now will enjoy further two holidays Saturday and Sunday. So, people are excited on Friday evening and usually celebrate it in their own ways. Some gathers in homes for dinner and whisky, others go out for dating, dinner and dance. The Dinner, restaurants, bars and dance clubs are very busy on Friday Evenings.

Summer: Summer lasts from June to August. These three months people are busy in outings. People travel a lot during summer at natural places of beauties in and outside America such as they go to beaches, sports events, sea travelling, water games, picnics, pool parties and so on. America is full of touring spots and places of natural beauties.

Other important Festivals

Christmas: Christmas is the most important festival in America. People spent lot of money on this festival. They spend money to buy new furniture, paintings, repair, decorating articles, gifts and even to setup their family life by getting family partners and go for other compromises.

4th July: 4th July is American Independence Day, they celebrate with pump and show in almost all-small and big cities. Lot of fireworks and musical programs are organized and performed in almost in all cities.

Father Day/Mother Day: To celebrate in the honor and love of parents. On these occasions children treat their parents with lunch/dinner and offer them lovable gifts.

Valentine's Day: This festival or custom is representing for loveable, where both treat each other will gift cards, presentations, outings and refreshing their love stories.

Martin Luther King's Birthday

Memorial Day

Labor Day

Veterans Day

Good Friday

President Day

Christmas Eve

Charismas Day

New Year Eve

Happy New Year

Important Agencies/Departments

For people living here, it has become a routine to deal with Federal and State Agencies (departments) on regular basis.

Commonly used Federal Agencies, specially for immigrants are:

Immigration & Naturalization Services (Immigration Department)

Internal Revenue Services (Tax Department)

Social Security Administration

Commonly Used State & Utilities Agencies:

Labor Department

State Division of Taxation

Commercial Recording State Division

County Office

Motor Vehicle Department

Bank Services

Utility Services Companies-Electric/Gas
Telephone Companies
Cable Services etc.

Economic System

America has adopted "Free Economy System", better known as "Capitalism". "Capitalism" is the opposite term of "Communism", two extreme contradictory economic terms (systems) available in current economic systems. Under "Communism" system most of the economic activities are dictated and control by the public sector, whereas under "Capitalism" most of the economic activities are controlled and developed by the private sector. Government does not control much except for licensing, compliance of rules & regulations, and tax collections etc.

It means by staying under compliance, one is free to perform any economic activity with no limit or restriction and can grow up to one's maximum capacity.

As for as economic activities are concerned you can advance horizontally or vertically. Vertically, for example, if you are a doctor, you can advance your medical practice upward or downward. Horizontally, same example, if you are a doctor, you can advance your business in other areas such as Motels, Hotels, and Manufacturing etc.

This is the reason, you can meet several business men, doing businesses in variety of areas. This has been possible even you do not have experience in other businesses, but still you can involve in them, because System & Training is available----commonly known as "Franchise Services."

America is secular country in theory and practice that means respect for all & every religion and is a casteless society. Therefore, discrimination based on religion, caste or color is neither allowed nor found.

But American culture is unique and different. The commonly used dress is Blue Jeans, T–Shirts and Snickers, though certain jobs require special dress codes and uniforms.

Being secular country, you have full freedom to maintain your culture, dressing and outlook. On the roads and in malls (big covered buildings having several stores under one roof) you can easily find several people wearing their classic country dresses and in their countries physical appearances.

Some people get their own complex and do not want to change to American way of dressing, while other believe do in Rome what Romans do, considering good for their professional success.

Political Environment

On the political side, Constitution has divided into three wings: -

1. Administration (Executive)-headed by President.
2. Legislation-headed by Congress.
3. Judiciary-headed by Supreme Court.

All the three wings are independent of each other, and they perform under their jurisdictions, rights and responsibilities as specified in the constitution.

President: Head of Administration:

Executive/Administration is headed by "President" in combination of President, Vice President and members of cabinet.

President is elected for four years. By convention till 1951 a person can stay as President for two terms. But twenty second amendment passed in February, 1951 has fixed this limit under act.

Understanding presidential election is little typical. I will try to explain in a simple way.

In USA, there are major two political parties, 1) Democrat Party and 2) Republican Party. In constitution, presidential election provision for an indirect election. Means voters of the nation will elect members of an Electoral College (total member 538) and those members of Electoral College will further elect a President and Vice President with majority vote. Electoral College has nothing else to do after electing the President. Electoral College is dissolved and its members will go home with no other political status or power.

So now what happened the political parties (the Democrats & the Republicans) start nominating their own candidates for electoral colleges' seats. If democrats are in majority, democrat candidate will be elected for President Position and if Republicans are in majority, republican candidate will be the President. On the ethic side those members of Electoral College do not change sides after their election to Electoral College. So presidential election has become virtually direct.

With passage of time, the concept of Electoral College remains with the political parties and constitutional bodies, and most of the general public somewhat forget about it. Political parties later realized that there is no need of putting candidates physically for Electoral College election because as a member of Electoral College and winning the seat as a member in the Electoral College, who virtually will have no job other than, electing the presidential candidate of his party. Better parties should not contest election for members of Electoral College, rather direct on president candidates, and no need individual members to contest for election.

The net result is a Presidential Candidate has to get majority in total Electoral College seats (jurisdictions) for which each State has been divided. Therefore, popular vote majority in USA seems irrelevant.

Perhaps this was the reason of dispute during the presidential election of 2000 between Mr. George W Bush & Mr. Al Gore and again in 2004 between Mr. George W Bush and Mr. John Kerry, of electoral seats v popular votes. Thus, it could be clear that a presidential candidate must enjoy majority of Electoral College seats to win the election. If a presidential candidate who secures majority in popular vote and as well as majority in Electoral College seats usually has no dispute. But a candidate who will have majority in popular vote but not majority in Electoral College seats, such situation may create confusion for some people, those who have no trail of original constitution and could be a case of constitutional interpretation.

Therefore, Presidential Election in USA is now practically is a direct election, but constitutionally it is still an indirect election.

President is mostly responsible for Administrating the country, implementation of the Laws & Foreign Policy.

Congress: Legislation

Congress is a combination of two houses—

1. House of Representatives- A Lower House.
2. Senate-An Upper House.
1. House of Representatives:

There are 435 members in House of Representatives who are elected by the voters of their 'Congressional District' for 2 years terms. They are called "Congressmen". Again, the House of Representatives is dominated by either of two parties' Democratic Party or Republican Party. New Jersey currently has 12 Congressional Districts out of total 435.

2. Senate:

Senate is the Upper House of" Congress" which has total of 100 members, as two members from each State irrespective of the area or population, and each member is elected for 6 years. The members of the senate are called "Senators".

The main role of the "Congress" which comprises of House of Representative & Senate is to make the laws. Each House has its own powers, procedures, election systems & terms those are out of scope to discuss in this book.

Members in Lower House are elected by voters of congressional directly. Lower House seems enjoying more powers in Legislation.

Judiciary-headed by Supreme Court

Supreme Court takes care of Judicial Systems & interpretation of Constitution as well as it is a highest Appellate institution in the USA Judiciary System.

America has Presidential System of Government and it differs with Parliament System of Government that exists, for example, in United Kingdom and India.

In Presidential system of government, president is not the representative of Congress (Parliament or lower house). Congress is independent of President that makes laws of its own where President has little or no influence or scope. Congress even can refuse some of President's actions to pass. If you remember that after First World War, UN was organized by American President but America was not its member because congress of USA did not approve USA to be its member. But in Parliamentary system where head of the Government is called Prime Minister is the representative of Parliament and enjoy majority in the say and rights. As well as head of State (Country) he will be the leader (head) of the Parliament and can enact any law he resolved. Parliament will support him/her in majority or he enjoys the majority in parliament. If compare both the position that of President and Prime Minister, a Prime Minister enjoys stronger positions than the President as far as comparison with regard to constitutional powers.

Apart from Federal Constitutional Structure, each State has its own constitution & Head of the State. The Head of the State is a Governor (an elected position) and State Legislation is called State Assembly (an elected body).

This political system has virtually no room for personal favors and influences in Government departments, Police, Tax Departments, Immigration and several other serving agencies. Government Office Administrations are easy, fast and corruption free. All-eligible office works are done quickly without any hassle. Accepting & offering bribe though is illegal by strict laws, but otherwise does not prevail in any department in theory & practice. It will be really hard to find a person, who can claim that he has got done his work by bringing any clerk or officer in any department. No one is above the Law in theory & practice.

Currency Valuation-Currently US dollar is very strong and stable. For example, USD is 75 times stronger than India Rupee-INR. Which means one USD is equal to 75 INR

Purchasing Power

Usually, every worker is able to make minimum of $2500/- a month. Dollar has very strong purchasing power, but certain items are very costly as well.

1. Apartment Rents:

Economy	$1000/month
Single Bedroom	$1300/month
Double Bedroom	$1800/month

2. Auto Insurance- $1000/up/year/liability

Other Costly Items—

Repairs

College Education

Medical Services

Grocery Items are of fresh & good quality available at very less prices.

Cup of Tea/Coffee	$2/up
Milk Gallon (3.785L)	$4/up
Coke cane	$1.50/up
Chicken	$2.00/lb.
Bear cane	$1.75/up
Whisky 1.75 liters-average brand	$30/up

Electronics items are in plenty & available at low prices—

Computer/Laptop	$ 500/up
TV	$500/up
Smart Phones	$500/up

Clothing: You can find lot of clothing on Sales in small & big stores---

Jeans	$30/up
T-shirt	$20/up
Petrol/Gas Gallon	$4/up

These figures are just approximate to give you some ideas. If an individual is making about $2500/month, he can have a normal life, and some room for savings. In the beginning it is a good idea to keep your expenses low to avoid financial tensions. People in the beginning manage their life economically, by sharing residents, buying stuff on sale, garage sale or used furniture & stuff. Anyhow expansion possibilities coupled with your efforts, can lead you soon towards comfortable life at quick speed.

Ultimately having car for each adult member, telephone connection in each room, TV in each room, separate computer for each member, separate bedroom for young members, variety of shoes and clothes etc. will be parts of the normal life, and spending goes with your income and life style.

America is a country of vast land approximately 3 times bigger than India, it is more on wider side, that east and west boarders have 3 hours' time difference. Population wise, its one fourth of India. Total population is 33 crores (330m)

Remember, it is charming to get departed from home to America, but as soon as you land USA, you will be fascinated by beautiful roads, buildings, and stores along with several confusions in your mind. You can easily imagine a deep ocean of struggle inside you as you can see a big challenge ahead. Your continued struggle, right and timely actions, direct focusing, can only make you succeed in proper settlement.

Your success mainly will depend on few of various factors:

- Kind of visa you have
- To whom you are arriving
- Your skill and education level
- Which town you are landing
- If any family/friend/employer support is available
- Money you carried with you
- Your personal excitement and attitude

It is like that, as you are in a big playground, where you will be creating your own game, playground and team up yourself. It is very easy to find people who are big success in a shorter period of time, whereas other could not make it even they are here for many years.

Your success will depend on your ability in exploring the opportunities, courage for availing, training for performing and developing skills to maintain and organize yourself.

Writing all about general life of people is out of scope of this book. This comes with long living experience.

Social Environment: Social environment is very open. There is no room for criticism and backbiting. The whole structure is to give and take respect. No one will bother you or care for your life style, eating habits, clothing, worshiping, marital status etc. I remember for the last 20 years, even no one has ever knocked my door. Further, it will depend on you how you want your social structure. You want a large social circle so you can develop. You want to live by yourself, no will bother you even your own relatives and friends. They will visit you only if you so want. Everyone is good in assessing your mood. Life is full of comfort and help from State agencies. Police itself is very helpful. So, you do not need to depend on social help much.

Business Environment

USA has adopted a capitalist economic system, which stands for free economy. Capitalism is an opposite term of Communism. In a communist type economy, most major business activities are controlled, managed and owned by the State (Government), and in a Capitalist Economy, most of business activities will be controlled, managed and owned mostly by the citizens and private sectors.

In such a system resources, production, prices, employment, income allocation etc. are determined by the interaction of market supply and demand, and where national economy tries to attain optimum level at faster speed.

There are merit and demerits of each system.

Most of the countries have adopted either or mixed economic system. In the modern era, I do not think, any country is following either system at extreme or pure level. But one can find some economies have more of Capitalism while other Communism/Socialism. Almost all-European, American and

Australian countries have more of capitalism system while Asian, African, And Arab countries have communism/socialism. The extreme example of pure Capitalism is USA and Communism is Russia and China.

These two types of economic giants had a long-time cold war among two groups. Each group was trying to influence and preach the world for the praise of their economic systems. Anyhow such a war does not seem to exist any anymore, perhaps everyone has realized that extreme of either system is not a good for economic development and for public life. Big compromises are going through out in all countries.

The developing countries have realized that communist way of economy is not efficient as compare to capitalist. Under a communist way, most of the business units are owned and managed by the government that is called "Public Sector" and such business units in capitalism are called "Private Sector".

Nations has found that public sector cannot produced efficiently due to State politics and lack of professional management systems, rather they are burden on their national economies. Government and politicians are more efficient in governing the laws and politics, but not good for managing businesses as typical businessmen and managers. Therefore, Government should set aside its interference and let the Private Sector should handle the business world except for major national ventures and overheads.

On the other hand, Public Sector is managed by the Government, therefore, workers and employees are highly protective against any exploitation. For this reason, public sector is considered more favorable in poor countries. On the other hand, Private Sector is in some ways are taken as very productive and may be subject to heavy exploitation, especially in poor countries.

India has adopted a midway that is called "Socialism". She has divided all the areas of business into three categories. First list contains the businesses which will be management by State (Public Sector) absolutely. Second list is for Private Sector. And the third is for joint ventures where government and private sector, both will participate. But even India has realized several economic weaknesses in the system and currently trying to enlarge the private sector.

American Capitalism: America has adopted a free economic system, which means any person can do any business at any level. He can explore the market, and set up any business anywhere. He will set up his plans, places, budget, timing and prices, and can grow as much as he wants or he can. By doing this he has to tackle economic issue himself like "competition". If he is free to do any business, so do others. You can beat others, and others can beat you based on prices, quality and marketing. You may survive, shine or sink, no one is there to stop you. Situation becomes like an ocean where bigger fishes can give tough time to smaller. Competition is at its peak. Ideas are caught, polished and introduced frequently. Marketing strategies are the key factors, which may be learned, borrowed or your own creations to be successful.

When I say "Free Economy" one should not conclude it to "Freedom". Federal State and local governments have setup tough rules and regulation to avoid exploitation, pollution and discrimination. They are at their toe to keep general public life a smooth and hassle free.

A few examples:

(1)   You may need a clearance from local government to open a particular business in a particular zone. You cannot open restaurant at a place you want. Area must be pre zoned for the purpose.

(2)   Special businesses such as liquor store, casino, bar, factory, industry etc. need special attention and licenses, and several other prerequisites to start such businesses.

(3)   There are rules for minimum wages, maximum hours of work. If one works more than the standard hours employer has to pay 1 ½ times of the wage.

(4)   Employer has to provide workers a set of standard benefits, such as Worker Compensation (Insurance for injury/disability), health insurance, unemployment insurance, old age benefits and medical benefits through social security system.

(5)   There are very strict rules against sexual harassment, child abuse and racial discrimination.

(6)   Consumers are protected through Consumer Affairs Department against any cheat with the customers and clients.

(7)   All the businesses have to maintain healthy environment at work places according to defined standards.

These are few examples. All such controls are true in theory and practice. So, the government is protecting the businesses in its own way.

Other way Government has very efficient way of taxation. Companies and their profits are controlled by tax brackets. More income more tax. That system encourages the small and big companies to expand and invest more in business. For examples big companies may plan or prefer to hire more people and pay more benefits or to expand the business instead of paying in taxes. The system has encouraged the development and expansion.

Even with all such strict rules and regulations, one does not feel any discrimination, corruption and uncomfortable in setting the business. All related agencies and departments are cooperative, helpful and efficient to perform their tasks on timely basis. State Governments, Federal Government, financial institutions and several non-profit organizations are there to help the small and new businesses.

One does not need any recommendation or bribing to any official for getting one's job done, because it is not there in theory and practice. Your all-official work will be done promptly without any hassle, if you are qualified, eligible and have proper documentation.

In conclusion you can do any business of course all lawful businesses, any anywhere and at any level by staying in regulatory compliance.

Regulatory compliance is crucial for all small or big businesses there is no exception or escape.

There is no limit on expanding your business. You can easily see the businesses those were very small one time and later they are at national and global level.

This manual will not cover business opportunities or business expansions. I will discuss certain steps to setup business in USA at initial level and basic knowledge that how to setup business and related tax issues in forth coming chapters.

Types of Business Entities

In USA businesses are organized under various types of entities. Each type of entity has its own merits and suitability, and off courses related demerits as well. The most common forms of entities are:

- Sole Proprietorship
- Partnership
- Corporation (Sub Chapter "S" Corporation/Regular "C" Corporation)
- LLC/LLP (Limited Liability Company/Limited Liability Partnership)

Out of all, Corporation setup is the most common and popular way being used for business ventures. I will give you brief discussion of each type of entity, and related benefits, with other characteristics and tax treatment of different types of entities.

I am briefly summarizing different features in forthcoming comparative study and you can very well get the idea of each type of entity.

- Sole Proprietorship v. Corporation
- "C" Corporation v. "S" Corporation
- LLC v. Corporation
- LLC v. Partnership

Caution: Before selecting a type of entity for your business, you must explore & consult for an appropriate type of entity for your business venture, because each type of entity has different features, suitable to different entrepreneurs based on:

- Kind of Business Venture.
- Short Term & Long Terms Goals
- Immigration Status
- Tax Treatments
- Legal Requirements
- Expansions Policies etc.

So that you should not have surprises later on, and modifications are either not possible or very complex. The discussion in this book is of basic in nature, and should not be used as a substitute of legal & professional advice.

Sole Proprietorship v. Corporation

Most of the businesses are done by individuals in their individual capacity, commonly known as "Sole Proprietorship" or "Sole-Practitioner" or "Self-Employed".

Sol-Proprietorship stands for the function that is performed in one's individual capacity. He brings his own idea and will start business activity almost with no or very less formalities.

Merits of Sole Proprietorship:

No requirements for formation or registering with State Department except you may have to register business name with the county office that is a very simple process.

No formalities are required such as Board Meeting or forming buy-laws. Sole Proprietorship will have his own business rules.

Sole proprietorship enjoys full authority and managerial control on his business.

Sole-Proprietorship can control business cost at individual level and at own decisions.

Sole proprietorship is good for small businesses in retail and service industries.

Opening, relocating or closing of business, is virtually simple in sole proprietorship set up.

Tax filing is simple, as the details of revenues, expenses and net profit is included on sole practitioner's personal tax return by using 'SECHEDULE - C (Form 1040) Profit or Loss from Business (Sole Proprietorship).

In certain situation, "one person control is always considered better, if that person is enough capable".

Sole Proprietorship business has to be in profit, as no one can afford losses in an individual capacity for long time. Therefore sole-proprietorship business has more probabilities of a profitable venture.

Local & State Governments, Banks, and several other agencies deal with small businesses, have several programs for the benefits of small businesses, where sole proprietor can mostly be eligible and benefited.

Sole Proprietorship can easily form their own local business associations for the mutual benefits and protection.

Business policies, customer services, diversions, pricing policies and other such issues are very flexible to amend in a sole proprietorship business to match with the current market requirement.

Demerits of Sole Proprietorship:

First thing, it does not have all features and benefits of a Corporation or any other type of entity established under separate legal entity concept. See Corporation later.

In a sole proprietorship owner is personally liable for all obligations and debts, and his, all or some personal assets are attached to business risk.

Business life is limited with the life of the sole proprietor that means business will die with the death of sole proprietor, unless is transferred to some one.

Sole proprietorship form of business is not good for expansions at different levels such as State, National or international levels.

Sole proprietorship does not attract professional employees or managers or may not afford professional management or advanced technical services.

Retaining employees may also be a problem for sole proprietor for lack of corporate benefit programs and corporate environment.

Sole proprietor entity may also be poor in attracting investors.

Expansion of business and business controlling activities may also be hard in sole proprietorship setup.

Sole proprietorship faces hard competition, and may be hard to afford professional & costly advertisements.

Sole proprietorship business is hard to reach at monopolistic level and earn super profit.

Corporation

Keeping in view the several benefits of Corporation structure, most of even small businesses, though they can function in sole proprietorship setup but still prefers to adopt Corporation structure. The consideration to setup a Corporation entity would be:

- Separate Legal Entity Concept.
- Perpetual Life
- Expansion Possibilities
- Attracting Investors and Lenders
- Protection of Personal Assets
- Attaining the professional management services
- Flexible Transferability of ownership

Demerits:

Corporation is a complex structure to setup and maintain:

- Complex legal formalities for filing and setup
- Complex formalities to maintain such as conducting various types of meetings and record keeping.
- Complex Tax Filing-Corporation has to file its own tax return and is a taxable entity (except for "S" Corporation which has to file its own tax return but is not a taxable entity, profit and loss pass through shareholders).
- Costly for registering, maintaining and tax preparation.

"C" v. "S" Corporation

New business setup seekers always come up with the question "What is the difference between "C" and "S" Corporation.

Usually we have regular type "C" Corporation and "C" Corporation is elected through an election process to be treated as an "S" Corporation.

"S" Corporation election process is with the IRS and State Tax Agency, that both allow a Corporation to be treated as "S" Corporation. So, we can say "S" Corporation is elected status for any "C" Corporation. That virtually makes two types of Corporations, i.e "C" and "S" with elected status Corporation. In more plain language "S" Corporation is an attained 'Status' of a regular 'C' Corporation through special election process, then it will enjoy a different tax treatment. Main difference would be in tax treatment.

"S" Corporation status is available subject to various restrictions and strict eligibility criteria; therefore, all Corporations will not find themselves eligible for the sub-chapter "S" Status.

Your business and expansion objectives also may not find "S" Status a better choice of your setup.

In general, "C" Corporation type entity itself is a taxable entity and it pays taxes on its earnings as per tax rates and tax brackets. It further means that "C" Corporation's net profit is subject to double taxation, at first at Corporation level, that pays tax on its net profit and again, at shareholders' level as personal income tax on distributed share of profit (dividend) of a Corporation.

Contrary to this sub-chapter "S" Corporation is not a taxable entity. Therefore, it does not pay taxes on its net income, though it has to file tax return annually on same pattern. Net income of an "S" Corporation is directly included and is taxable to individual shareholders in their stock percentage, irrespective of the fact whether they have received their share (dividend) or not. If taken in later year(s), such distribution of prior paid taxes, will not be taxed.

In case of loss, a "C" Corporation carries its losses itself for certain duration to set off from its future profits.

An "S" Corporation's loss is directly passed over to the shareholders in their respective proportion of his share in business that they can set off from other personal incomes or carried forward whatever could be applicable.

An "S" Corporation has better tax treatment, but there are several eligibility requirements and restrictions to be qualified for an "S" Corporation Status.

A Corporation will be qualified for an "S" Status if it is:

- A domestic Corporation
- Has 100 or less shareholders
- Has no shareholder other than individuals, an estate or certain tax-exempt organization
- Has no non-resident alien as a shareholder-foreign investor.
- Has only one class of shares
- Is not prohibited statutorily.
- An "S" Corporation Status (election) has been applied within due time limits.

It means a foreign Corporation, or having more than 100 shareholders, or having more than one class of shares, or having a non-resident alien as a shareholder etc, will be a disqualification for "S" Corporation status. And the election must be applied with in due time for current consideration, otherwise future options can be availed.

Even a Corporation which is qualified for "S" Corporation and elect to be an "S" Corporation, and in future if either of fact, if happen, can make it disqualified and it will be "C" Corporation. For example, if number of shareholders in an "S" Corporation exceeds 100 any time in future or non-resident shareholder(s) joins, its "S" Corporation status can be terminated. It means a Corporation should be eligible for "S" Corporation, not only at the time of election, rather it has to maintain its status with same terms and restrictions to keep enjoying its "S" Status all the times.

Choice for "C" Corporation.

Though "S" Corporation is a better choice still some Corporations may not opt for "S" Corporation status, though otherwise they may be eligible.

Reason they do not find "S" Corporation as a suitable entity according to their current business venture or future plans.

Here are few examples. Corporation has serious plan to keep reinvesting its earning for expansions for number of years and will not distribute its profit to its owners (shareholders). As shareholders will not receive share of profit (dividend), they will not have taxable dividend income. Corporation will be taxed, but Corporation tax rates are low as compared to personal tax rates. Contrary to it "S" Corporation's profit share is taxable to individual shareholder whether they receive the dividend or not. In a situation, a Corporation can plan to remain as a "C" Corporation.

Corporations those have plans to expand their businesses in other Countries (international level) and plan to include non-resident shareholders for investment *or* other purposes, may not find an "S" Corporation as a suitable entity under their future business plans..

A Corporation who has planned to issue different classes of shares to attract different kind of investors so that they can generate the capital from maximum sources, will also prefer not to opt for an "S" Corporation Status.

In brief, having "C" Corporation may be a business choice or due to non-eligibility for "S" Status

Some Special Features of C: Corporation:

Advantages:

- Separate legal identity: Available in some other entities
- Limited liability for the owners
  Available in some other entities
- Perpetual existence
  Available in some other entities
- Separation between ownership and management
- No restrictions on who can hold shares: No restriction of Visa or Citizen of Foreign Countries.
- Readily transferable shares
- Well-established legal precedents
- Widespread acceptance by the venture capitalists and other investors
- Ability to offer stock options
- Can issue different types of Shares
- Good to go Public
- Expanding possibility for National & International
- Easy for diversion of business line.
- High employees' benefit plans.
- Can hold the retain earning for growth
- Tax rates are generally lower than the personal rates
- Good for Accrual Basis Tax Filing.
- It carries, forwarded the losses itself.
- Tax planning opportunities
- Professional Management.

It has some disadvantages as well:

- Double taxation. The C Corp is taxed at the corporate level, and the owners of the company are taxed on dividends paid from the Corporation. Therefore, the Corporation will pay corporate income tax, and the owners and shareholders will pay personal income tax on such dividends.

- C Corps are generally regulated more so than other types of entities. as C Corps must hold a number of regular events such as periodic meetings, including board meetings and regular shareholder meetings. Meeting minutes from each of these meetings are also required to be kept on file.

- Government oversight of C Corps is greater due to the complex tax laws and higher protection provided to shareholders of such Corporations.

LLC v. Corporation

LLC (Limited Liability Company) is an entity, which also enjoys separate legal entity concept. LLC has the features in combination of partnership and of a Corporation. Owners of LLC are called "Members" and in a Corporation, they are called "Shareholders". Shareholders of a Corporation and Members of an LLC have limited Liability and protection of personal assets.

LLC is more flexible entity for changing profit and loss rations of its members (owners). In a Corporation, once the shares and stocks are issued, they established a sort of permanent ratio, unless a shareholder himself or herself surrenders or sells their shares. On the other hand, shareholder can transfer or sell their share virtually at their discretion, but in LLC, members may not enjoy such flexibility that is good to avoid entrance of unwanted member (partner) in the company.

LLC is good in the sense that it has features of partnership and flexible in profit and loss ratios.

LLC is not a taxable entity, and does not pay taxes, rather its profit and loss passes directly apportioned to its members in their respective sharing ratio, that is further included in their personal tax returns. For tax purpose it files 'Partnership Tax Return'. But it can opt to be treated as a Corporation for filing its tax return. In such a case, it will file Corporation tax return.

An LLC can have single Member (only one owner) or Multiple Members (two or more partners): Both use different Tax-Forms to file their annual Tax Returns. Single Member LLC is by default a sole-proprietor that files IRS Form 1040 with Schedule "C". Multiple Members LLC is by default a Partnership that file Partnership Tax Return IRS Form 1065.

A single member LLC cannot file partnership tax return; therefore, it will file its annual tax return either as a sole-proprietor or can opt to be treated as Corporation for Tax Return filing purpose.

In comparative study with "C" Corporation and "S" Corporation, LLC has mixture of features of both. For example, LLC can include non-resident members and entity other than individuals as is possible in "C" Corporation but not in "S" Corporation. For Tax purpose a "C" Corporation is a taxable entity and pays taxes on its profit, whereas LLC like an "S" Corporation is not a taxable entity and does not pay taxes on its profit, rather like "S" Corporation, its profits and losses are passed to its members.

To setup LLC, one has to follow registration requirement almost similar to a Corporation. For a Corporation "Article of Association" is filed with the Secretary of State and for LLC "Article of Organization" is filed with the Secretary of State. Filing cost and filing fee etc can be considered almost same.

LLC can be managed by Partnership Operating Agreement" and a Corporation by both, "Agreement(s)" and "By-laws"-a set of rules of a Corporation or a Constitution of a Corporation.

An LLC type of entity, has fewer requirements in comparison of a Corporation associated with various types of formalities. A Corporation has to follow various and strict procedural formalities to maintain its Corporation status with regards to various periodical Board Meetings and Shareholder Meetings, and Management Procedures.

Capital structure wise, Corporation is a better choice that can issue different types and classes of shares and debt instruments to attract different types of investors and management choices and eventually can go for public trading. A normal LLC has to depend on members' contributions and debt or borrowed funding.

LLC v Partnership

Like sole proprietorship, general partnership is another entity that is easy to setup. There are no legal requirements for registrations except it may have to register business name with the county office. It is an association of two or more people to join a business venture for profit and can be organized by mutual agreement and understanding. It is also governed by common law of the State for partnership entities. Partnership type entity is easy to dissolve with mutual consent, or automatically upon death of a partner, resigning of a partner, completion of the venture or project or completion of the term.

Like sole proprietorship, partners are personally liable for partnerships' obligations and debts. They do not enjoy the feature of LLC or of a Corporation of limited liability and protection of personal assets.

An LLC, in that sense is a better choice though it involves legal registration process. The members enjoy the features of limited liability and protection of personal assets. An LLC has features of both of a Corporation and Partnership, therefore it can serve the purpose of both except for tax treatment and long-term business plans.

Tax filing could be the same, if LLC chose and eligible for filing partnership tax return. Both will file the same type and same style of tax return that is "Partnership Tax Return". General Partnership and LLC are not taxable entities and its profit and loss pass through to its members.

The admin functioning & management of an LLC and of a Partnership can be managed through mutual agreement.

Dissolution of LLC will require reporting and following of certain legal and tax formalities, whereas Partnership can be dissolved or terminated by without any legal formalities except for filing final tax return.

Separate Legal Entity Concept

Some Business entities like Corporations, LLCs etc. , will exist separately from its owners. In a common language that a Corporation is a separate entity from of its owners or it is a separate artificial person and owners are the real persons. A Corporation is a combination of two persons, one itself Corporation as an artificial person and its owners as real persons. In accounting, this concept exits in almost all kinds of business entities.

A Corporation lives and does its activities at its own existence and is treated in its own capacity. It does the business, it generates the revenue, it can incur losses, it hires the employees and it pays its own taxes.

It is a better form of existence for the reason it takes its responsibilities itself, owners are free from their personal liabilities and owners enjoy limited personal liability (risk) only up to their investments in stocks, though there may be certain situations where their personal responsibilities can exceed from limited liability concept in case of legal determinations, such as violations & gross negligence.

Separate entity concept is a better choice and it has better features because Corporation enjoying separate entity concept, has indefinite life (perpetual). Management and ownership may change but Corporation will exist indefinitely at its own existence, unless it is officially dissolved or merged.

Corporation has a better scope for large and multiple businesses, expanding business, securing debts, attracting investors, retaining professional setup and engaging professional management, promoting and achieving new ideas, expanding its activities at local to global level.

Under Separate Entity Concept, Corporation is treated in its own capacity, but it is not a human being, it is an artificial being, therefore, it has to be managed by people in different capacities such as owners, directors, managers or employees, those are supposed to work ethically and represent it in their vested authorities. Corporation seal is used for Corporation signature on important and legal documents

Limited Liability Concept:

Corporations & some other registered entities enjoy the Limited Liability Concept, that means shareholders or members or owners will be responsible only up to their interment in case business venture is collapsed. Their personal assets will be secure from any dispute. Borrowers etc can sue against the assets of the Entity, but not of its Shareholders or owners' personal assets to satisfy the debt of business. This concept is known as "Corporate Veil", means owners are behind the curtain.

But some time: Piercing the corporate veil can happen where owners of a Corporation losing the limited liability that was given in Corporation type setup. Actually this can happen with the Court

Order where Owner(s) is in willful gross negligee or due to his/their fraudulent activity. When this happens, the owners' personal assets can be used to satisfy business debts and liabilities.

Corporation: Setting up process:

Corporation is one of the output of several types of business entities. Its creation involves a statutory required processing with Secretary of State, Department of Commercial Recording by filling article of Association and paying statutory fee.

Article of Association is a legal document which contains the:

- Name of Corporation
- Business Address
- Purpose of Corporation
- Information about Initial Director(s)
- Information about registered agent.
- Registered Office Address
- Authorized number of shares
- Types or classes of shares
- Other article's provisions

"Article of Association" is public record information and name of such entity should have proper designation to understand entity as a 'Corporation' such as

- Inc.
- Incorporated
- Corp.
- Corporation
- Ltd.

Corporation can have a name of its choice subject to availability with the State of Incorporating. In State each Corporation should have unique and different name to avoid the conflict with other Corporation having similar name. You may have to follow name availability search or to get name reservation services to adopt a specific name of the Corporation.

The successful filing of articles of association gives the birth to a "Corporation" in the name specified therein.

Business Setup process

Remember Business Registration is a subject matter of each State and of Federal Government. You will be deciding in which State you like to do this business apart from your residential choices. Each State will have different advantage and facilities to attract the businesses. Which is a good State, it will depend on your type of business. Otherwise, each State is good for one or other reason. Because, the filing or incorporating business is a State-subject, therefore, filing procedure and filing fees will differ State to State.

Once you know the different types of options of business entities available, you should be able to find the most suitable entity for your business venture. I will give you the complete setup of cycle of each type of entities.

Sometime your options are limited under business laws and your immigration status. For living and working in USA, you also need an appropriate immigration status as well. For example, you are a foreign Corporation and want to setup business in USA, you may setup "C" Corporation only, because "S" Corporation type entity does not allow foreigners to be the stock holder. In such an event "S" Corporation will lose its "S" Corporation status and will become "C" Corporation. A foreign Corporation can setup its branch in USA, that will be known a foreign entity or alternatively they can setup a domestic Corporation having ownership interest. Such an entity will be considered a "Subsidiary" of parent company.

Setting up Sole Proprietorship (Self practitioner): Setting up sole proprietorship is very easy and simple, that does not require much legal formalities.

Name Registration: If you are deciding to do business under your own name, you do not need to register your business anywhere. But if you pick up a business name other than yours own, you have to visit County office of the jurisdiction, where you are setting your business to register the business name. Registration of business name is just easy, that one may have to visit in person in county office and has to search availability of name of your choice, and most of record is in the shape of old ledgers and registers. County staff will let you search the name. If the name of your choice is not taken by any others business, or is available, you can file registration at the spot. There is filing fee and little paper work. In these days most of the services are also available on line on your jurisdiction county sites.

Note: If you plan to do sole proprietorship in other counties as well, you may have to register business names in other counties also.

Note: Counties are different segments of a State. A State is divided into several counties, counties in districts and districts in cities and towns.

Partnership: Same way you do not need to registration for partnership entity. But if you want to do business under name other than your own name you may have to register the name in your local county and in all other counties where you will be conducting business. Name registration process is the same, as of sole proprietorship.

Caution: When you select a unique business name for your venture, you cannot use mis-designation after business name such as "Inc" "Corp" or "LLC". Such Designations are available only State Registered Entity.

Corporation:

Corporation is considered the most suitable business form for local, national and international businesses, and small to global level businesses. Setting a Corporation is highly legalized process, one may need a good professional help to setup a Corporation and maintain its corporate status. Before you start up setting. You may have to decide for several issues such as initial director (s), registered agent, registered office, number and types of shares to be authorized and incorporates etc. Because once the Corporation is setup, changing or amending options are complicated and need additional filing processes and fees as well. Moreover, you have also to decide whether you want to setup "C" Corporation or "S" Corporation subject to eligibility.

Next Step will be name search: Corporations are registered with Secretary of State. Each State has its own registration process, and commercial recording department. If proposed name of your Corporation is available in the State where you want to setup your Corporation, you can follow the next step.

Note: Even the proposed name of your Corporation is available, it can be taken away by others before you submit your filing papers. It is good to reserve the proposed name if name of the Corporation is special and you are serious about it.

All States have their own name search systems. Better way to call the commercial recording department, they will help you to find name search for you. Some States charge fee for name search and name reservation. Some States have database on their web sites to complete the name search.

If you are not yet ready to file the Corporation article, but worried about the name of Corporation that should not be taken by others, you can reserve the name by paying name reservation fee. Under this process your name will be secured for you for 30-60 days.

Next Step will be preparation of "Articles of Incorporation" or **"Articles of Organization-LLC".** Articles of Incorporation is legal document) containing several clauses and articles relating to a Corporation. Each type of Corporation may have different articles and clauses. "Articles of Incorporation" is like a Birth Certificate of a Corporation that will contain several articles as indicated in earlier chapters.

Once the draft is ready, it is sent to commercial recording unit of State in which you planned to do the business along with the filing fee. The Secretary of State will register the article and you will get "filing copy" and Corporation certificate. Your Corporation is now on public record and is now legally setup and is ready to act. Now a days almost all States have on-line setup process.

Note: Setting Corporation or any entity is really complicated, and I strongly suggest to seek legal or professional advice before hand and better to hire some professional for setting your business in legal and complete setup sense. The information being given is to give you introduction and basic knowledge.

In these days most States web portals are available such as in New Jersey, entities: Corporation/LLC etc. can be register on line: link will be given later, and have simple incorporation/organization process, but still, you should explore/consult for proper suitable entity, and additional classes to be enter in your online Certificate of Corporation/Certificate of Organization.

Doing Business in Multiple States:

USA has 50 States and a Corporation can do business only in the State in which it is registered or incorporated. If a Corporation wants to do business in other State(s), it can do so only upon registration the same Corporation in other State(s) where it wants to expand the business. The process is all most same. The Corporation will prepare and file "Articles of Incorporation" or will apply for "certificate of authority" and upon successful filing it will be known as "foreign Corporation" in those State(s) (as all 50 States of US are basically different countries). The process is also known as getting Certificate of Authority to do the business in other States.

For example, you setup Corporation in New Jersey (One of the 50 States of USA), and later same Corporation wants to do business in other State as well, say Georgia. Now the New Jersey Corporation has also to file article of association as a foreign corporation in Georgia and to get Certificate of Authority in Georgia. Thus, this Corporation will be known as Foreign Corporation in Georgia and Domestic Corporation in New Jersey. In such a process there may be problem of name availability in other State(s). If the same name is not available in any other State, Corporation may have to pick up other name of its choice again subject to availability. So, a Corporation can do business under different name(s) in other States.

More than One Corporation: A common question comes all the time, whether a person can setup more than one Corporation. Answer is yes. Not only a Corporation but other entities subject to fulfilling eligibility terms as specified by each State. For example, a person can have 5 Corporations, 4 LLCs' and 6 sole proprietorships etc. Not only a person, but also a legal entity such Corporation and LLC can have other Corporations. Such relations are known parents-subsidiaries corporate structure. Only issue will be with accounting aspects. This book will be covering only basic information and not complex structures.

Can a Corporation do more than one business: Corporation can do more than one business of course lawful businesses. Only formalities are left that each business has to complete licensing and other required formalities.

'DBA' Name: DBA stands for "Doing Business As" It is also called alternate name. This is another attractive feature where a Corporation or LLC can do its business by using name other than its own. This is a common type of feature in USA business world. This required for so many reasons where Corporation name is not appropriate for the type of business venture, or same Corporation want to do several businesses at a time. For example, XYS, Inc. wants to do business of fast-food restaurant, clothing retail store, shoe store, jewelry stores and so on. Now they can pick up different alternate names for each type of business such as Ashoka Diner, Riva Jeweler, BMC Shoe Store and so on.

But be sure Corporation itself will be responsible for consolidating the accounts and filing tax returns. DBA names are only for business conducting purpose and they do not create separate entities.

How to get DBA name: Once a Corporation is setup, one can apply for DBA name registration. Application form (NJ: C-150G) is simple and filing fee is there. You can file DBA names as many as you want, but they will be valid for certain period (5 years in New Jersey) unless you keep renewing them.

Doing several businesses under one Corporation: Is it a good idea?

Not really. It is simple for accounting and tax filing purpose. But may not be good from limited liability point of view. Liability cf a Corporation is limited to its assets. For example, if one business got liability problem, it will impact the other businesses of the same Corporation. By doing different businesses under different Corporation may reduce this kind risk.

LLC (Limited Liability Company). This is another form of business entity under separate legal entity concept that also requires registration process with the State as well. The process is almost in the same pattern as of a Corporation. One has to go for name search and preparation and filing of Article of Organization. (For Corporation it is known as Article of Association).

Federal Tax ID: The next important step is to apply for Federal Tax ID. It is also known as EIN (Employment Identification Number). Federal Id is indispensable for doing business in USA. IRS (Federal Tax Agency) monitors the business activities through EIN. If you are a sole proprietor, you may skip this process as you may do business under your own social security number. But if you want to hire employees and pay them wages, even sole proprietorship has to obtain this number. You can apply Federal Tax ID by using form 'SS-4: Application for Employer Identification Number' paper and on line form is simple to file, but still, I suggest to consult some professional, before filing it, as it asks for several important information such as accounting period and closing month etc.

A Business whether it is a Corporation or LLC or any other entity, will need Federal Tax ID for almost every purpose, such as opening bank account, filing payroll, filing income taxes, signing leases, getting licenses and other registrations, signing business contracts. Businesses are recognized by their names as well as Federal Tax ID. Business to Business word Federal Tax ID is called by several names such as EIN, Tax ID, Tax Number, ID, Federal ID etc. Tax ID is a standardized of 9- digits unique number assigned to each business entity (00-0000000).

State Tax ID: Once a business is assigned with federal ID, business has to register business with State Taxation/Finance department also. Each State has its own format to apply for State ID and business registration. A Business will also need State ID for filing and paying State taxes, payroll taxes and paying sales tax. Sometime people get confused with the process. They think that once the Corporation is registered with State, why to register the business again. But see, Corporation filing is not typical registering of the business. The process is just to incorporate the business that create a legal entity for commercial record and public information. Business registration is a different that is with the State Tax and Finance departments and allow the Tax department to get all details of business such as location of business, type of entity, nature of business, accounting period, number of employees, owners' information, and other relevant details. If a corporation is registered in other State as a foreign Corporation, it has to apply for State Tax ID (account number) and State Registration with all such States as well.

Sales Tax ID/Authority to Collect the Sales Tax: If your business is of retail type, you may also have to apply for Sales Tax ID and Sales Tax Authority Certificate.

Licenses: You may need other licensing depending on the nature of your business or if so required, such as Cigarette License, Fuel License, Liquor License, Lotto License, Milk License, Fast Food License, Bear License and so on. Such licenses are issued by different agencies to eligible businesses. To get such licenses there may be several eligibility requirements and will involve filing process and filing fees. Some licenses are normal to get and some will be very complicated and one may have to go through hard eligibility and filling criteria. For example, getting Liquor License needs highly regulatory process. To find out which licenses you need, which agency is concerned and what will be the procedure, better you contact local county office, consumers affairs department and secretary of State Secretary of State.

County Clearance: Before you start any business in any county/city better to consult and contact the local city office to know whether particular business is allowed in a particular building or area. So, you may need Certificate of Occupancy from the local government office, Zoning Certificate, Fire Inspection, Health Certificate and some other.

Note: It is always a good idea to contact local county office before you sign any lease to find out that particular site is permitted for desired business venture.

Processing for "S" Corporation: If Corporation has decided for "S" Status and is also eligible, it should do so at its earliest, because there is time limit of 75 days. This process is also two tiers. Corporation has to apply for "S" Corporation with Federal (IRS) and with the State Taxation Department. Keeping in mind that if Corporation is registered with other State(s) as a foreign Corporation, it may be filing "S" Corporation in other those States as well. If one Corporation cross this dead line, then it can still apply but it will be effective from next accounting year. There is a process to get retrospective 'S' status by paying additional fees, see if it is available in any desired case. There are specified application forms for applying for "S" status with Federal and States.

For IRS Form is IRS-2553: Election by a small business Corporation.

For New Jersey is CBT-2553: New Jersey S Corporation Election

Summary: Steps to Set "S" Corporation: As an S Corporation is a single taxable entity a large number of businesses are attractive to get this status, keeping in view its special popularity, and better tax treatment.

Steps for Eligible Corporations

First Register Your Business as a Corporation:

There is no direct "S-Corporation" registration, rather subchapter "S" Corporation status can be acquired, if any Corporation, is eligible and also desires to opt for.

- First Register a Corporation or incorporate a business.
- Get a Federal ID: Use SS-4 Form-Application for Employer Identification Number. On-Line Application is also available on IRS-site.
- Get a State ID: Different Form for each State. For example, for New Jersey: Form: NJ-Reg-Business Registration Application.

On-Line Application is also available on New Jersey State-web-site.

- Apply for an S Corporation Status:
- Use IRS Form 2553: Election by small business Corporation.
- Use New Jersey Form CBT 2553: New Jersey S Corporation Election.
- Send them for approval on given address within permitted time
- Expect Receive Approval/Acceptance in 6 weeks.
- There is no fee for applying for "S" Corporation status

Note: Covering only New Jersey State, as covering of all States is out of scope of this book.

It will be effective from the current tax year or next year as approved or accepted.

Bank Account

Your next step should be to open the bank account. You can open bank account in the name of business in any bank or in any number of accounts. IRS desires that business transactions should be maintained separately than the personals, therefore, mixing business transactions with personal bank account is not a good idea. It is needed that business accounts should be maintained separately and should contain all and only business transactions. But business can open as many accounts as needed such as:

Main Checking Account: Two conducted main business transactions.

Payroll Checking Account: Two conducted transactions relating to payroll and payroll taxes.

Money Market Account: To accumulate savings.

Certified & Fixed Deposit Accounts: To secure business savings and surplus cash for fixed period of terms.

Or you can manage the whole business simply through one account. Most commonly such an account is known as "Main Business Checking Account". Checking account means that account is operated through the transmissions of Checks (Cheques). Because most of the payments are paid via checks, so business needs checking account.

How to open a Bank Account: Process is simple. Each bank has professional customer services and helps to open bank account. But generally, to open a corporate bank account, Corporation has first to pass the resolutions to opening a bank account with majority of the shareholders and has to decide the signing authorities. Most of the Banks in USA has a resolution format, only shareholders or authorized director have to sign and stamp with Corporation seal.

For some Corporation selecting the signing authorities are sometime very crucial, specially where there is more than one owner. On the other side giving signing authority for banking purpose is also a matter of trust and integrity. You can consider several options keeping in view the suitability of the business and convenient of transactions, such as:

Only one person should sign the checks

Two or more person should sign the check (jointly)

Either of two or more person can sign the check

Up-to certain amount one person's signatures are enough, over and above two or more will sign and so on.

Selecting a Bank: Sometime it is not an easy process. Keeping in view the nature of your business and your financial needs, one may have to explore and negotiate a lot to find a suitable bank. For ordinary business or to start with, you can pick up any brand name commercial bank. But if your business is really typical such as Wholesale Diamond Corporation who has clients all over the USA and vendors in foreign countries, may need wire transfer service, overdraft, credit lines, invoice factoring, bank letters, bank guarantees, commercial loans and other typical services all the time. All the bank may not provide these services or may be very conservative. And more over these services will cost you several bank service-charges. In such a situation one may have to struggle to find the right bank having such services at reasonable rates.

Note: It is always a good idea to consult similar type of businesses about the banking recommendation if you know people and businesses similar to yours and then try negotiate your own terms in selecting suitable Checking Account Package or Type.

Filing Requirement for a business in the State:

Almost all kind of businesses has one or other kind of filing requirements. Most Common Requirements are:

1. Income Tax return filing: Annual: With IRS and all States, in which business is registered and/or being conducted. Even some States have filing requirement even for businesses with zero income: or no business activity or even business is inactive status. And they may have the requirement of minimum tax amount. On the contrary there are some States those do not have State Income Tax for Individuals and/or Businesses.

2. Annual Reporting: This mostly apply on registered entities like Corporation, S Corporation, LLC or any other registered entity.

   Difference between Annual Tax Return filing & Annual Report:

1. Both are annual filing.

2. Filing dates are different: Tax Filing becomes due from each January for prior calendar year for calendar year filers whereas Annual Report is due by each year of the month company was registered.

3. Tax Filing is due to Taxation Department: Annual Report is due to Commercial Recording Department.

Common Insurances for Businesses: There are several kinds of insurances you may need to run your business; mostly will depend on the nature of your business. Some are being discussed as follow:

* Mandatory
* Optional
* Optional but commonly used
* Optional but forced by outside parties
* Optional but good to control damage and so on.

Workers' Compensation and General Liability Insurance:

Workers' Comp Insurance: This "Insurance" is mandatory for each employer who has one or more employee(s) for protection of your employees. However monthly premium of Employers Workers' Compensation, will depend on nature of your business with risk factor code and total amount of wages paid in each year.

General Liability: This may be optional, but may be pressed by your clients, customers, landlord, other outsiders and circumstances.

Almost all Corporations and other businesses are required to maintain these insurance policies. Workers' Comp Insurance protects the employees against any miss-happening and General Liability Insurance protects the customers and clients. For getting these insurances, again, one has to shop around a lot, because different agencies may have different premium rates. Other important factor to keep in mind is that insurance agencies should be able to understand your nature of business properly. Each type of business has its own insurance code, and premium is determined according to that code. For example, manufacturing business will be insured under the manufacturing code. Manufacturing is more risky business for employees, so insurance premium will be more. But contrary to it service business has little risk it will be assigned different code for lessor premium. For example, Software Consulting and Software Development may be assigned different code. If you are a Software Consulting company which is purely a service business and instead an insurance agency, consider it as a Software Development, this misunderstanding may cause you to pay a high premium.

Premium for workers' comp. insurance will depend on the total number of employees, outside employees, (sub-contractor not insured their own) inside employees, their functions, location of employees and total payroll cost for each year. Every year Insurance Company sends their auditors to audit the payroll record and determines the premium.

Other Insurances:

- Error & Omission Insurance
- Professional Labilities Insurance
- Rental Insurance
- Home Insurance
- Vehicle Insurance: for your business vehicles
- Medical Group Health Insurance: A perk for your employee
- Key-Employee Insurance
- Fire Insurance
- Life Insurance-with limit: as perk to employees
- Transit Insurance….and so on.

Other Start up formalities: The further formalities may vary business to business depending upon the nature of business. The best thing is that one can join business associations, chambers of commerce and other business groups and to attend their meetings. Such associations are the best source of all pertaining information to know and discuss new ideas and updates.

Setting Office

Generally, one further needs to setup office, store, warehouse or any kind of real estate. Leasing for business space is also a little tedious matter. One may need legal consulting before signing any lease agreement, because once the lease agreements are signed, you cannot back out without the consent of landlord. Most of the lease contracts are drafted by the attorney's representing landlords and therefore, those may be more for protecting them. To counter and to understand the complications of lease agreement one has to consult or retain legal professional for lease agreement.

Not only for 'lease contract', but if your business involves lot of contractual businesses, you should have an attorney on permanent basis.

Similarly foreign Corporations may need legal help for immigration services for their officers and employees. Setting up business is one thing and staying in this country in compliances is other. To stay and work in this country in any capacity, one may also need an appropriate visa. Immigration processing is pretty complex. A small mistake at initial level can be a big issue for long term immigration benefits. Therefore, in such a situation you should have an attorney for immigration purpose.

Some attorneys are good for immigration matters whereas other for corporate matters, and some are good for both. So, before retaining an attorney you must assess your needs and the expertise of the attorney.

Similarly, you may need an accounting professional most appropriate professional is known as Certified Public Accountant in USA and, as Charted Accountant in some other countries. Tax and new complete business setup are also pretty complex and complicated. A professional CPA can help you to organize your accounting and tax affairs and can help you to pick up right entity of business setup based on taxation and accounting.

Organizing business place: Organizing business place that include installing of telephone lines, internet, ordering furniture, gas electric connections, cleaning services etc. is very easy. All such agencies are listed in the phone book of the area known as "Yellow Pages". You can get these services just by calling them. All agencies are prompt and efficient in providing quick service. Gas, electric or other State agencies have fixed rates, but phone companies have different rate for different packages. You may have to explore with them about the package which is suitable to your business needs and any promotional rates are available.

Hiring Employees.

Hiring Employees comes under Human Resource Functions (HR) of a business. I will not discuss the total function of HR. But hiring employees is the major part of a business. If you need to hire employees for your business, this chapter can be very important for you. This will give you preliminary information about the hiring process.

Types of Employees:

Basically, employee is an employee. But for certain hiring policies they fall into different categories such as:

Full time employee

Part Time Employee

Permanent Employee

Temporary employee

Consultant

Clerical

Officer

Manager

Salesperson

Contractor etc.

HOW TO SETUP BUSINESS IN USA

But basically, employees fall in **two major** categories as per IRS-Internal Revenue Service-Federal Tax Agency:

W2 employees and

1099-Workers: Sometime they are called 1099-Employees, but mandatory they are Independent Contractors.

W2 Employees: W-2-Wage and Tax Statement is an IRS recognized Tax-form which must be issued to all the employees who are on the payroll. W-2 is the name of solid document which clearly indicates that the recipient is an employee & has employee & employer relationship. This document contains the information about the gross wages given to an employee during a year, tax withholding and other deductions and additions of certain benefits. Because an employer has to issue W-2 form to all its employees, therefore, such employees are known as 'W-2 employees'.

1099-Workers: Contract/Contractor Employees: If any employer hires an employee on a contract basis, at the end of year, he will issue him a tax document known as Form 1099-NEC-Nonemployee Compensation, which will be the proof that the recipient is an independent contractor and not an employee, and does not have an employee-employment relation. This document will contain the information of total compensation or other payment made to him during the year, and will help him to file his yearend tax return.

Both the documents are important to each type of employee, because employees prepared and file their personal tax return based on the financial information and tax withholding on these documents.

W2 V. 1099

Anyhow, there is a fundamental difference between W2-Employees and 1099-Workers or Employees, and an employer is not free to put any employee in either category. IRS has set very strict guidelines.

Treating a W2-Employees as 1099 Worker is subject to heavy penalties to an employer.

W-2 Employees: Almost all employees who work in your premises and supervisory control should be W2 employees. The brief definition is if some someone works in your premises, under supervision and directions, then he is an employee. But IRS has setup 20-Factor-Test for employers caution to determine someone 1099-Employee. Actually there is no official term known as 1099-Employee. This term is used in layman language. 1099-Workers are best suitable for contract jobs not as employees.

1099-Workers: Basically, they are called sub-contractors or self - employed or independent contractors, and they work for you to accomplish the task given by you according to their own way without the employer's supervision or time control for a set (contract) price, can only be a sub-contractor, contractor or self-employed working for you.

Note down few examples: Your secretary, book-keeper, HR Manager, Office Clerk, Store Manager etc are your employees because they work under the employer's supervision and directions. Treating them as a 1099-Workers will be a violation of IRS "20-Factor-Test" But a mechanic who comes to fix your air-condition system, a painter who comes to paint your office, a mechanic to fix your network for a contract price is typically not your employee. But treating a person as a 1099-contractor whereas he should be treated as W-2 employee as per 20-Factor Test is a big concern.

In USA it is a common practice to have sub-contractors and employees to get the work done. But some time, it becomes hard to determine whether a worker should be taken as 1099-Worker or W2-Employee. But before you treat some someone as sub-contractor you must go through the IRS guidelines or consult your CPA. Because treating a sub-contractor as your employee may not be any hassle, but treating an employee as sub-contractor is big issue. Because there is a major difference between payroll tax treatment for W2-employees and 1099-Workers. Some Employers are tending to prefer to hire some employee as 1099-Workers. Because an employer does not pay its matching share of Social Security & Medicare Tax in respect of 1099-Workers and other statutory benefits and because of some assignment can easily be classified either.

For example: An Accountant, if working on your business site under your supervision is an employee but if he is working from his own office, is a Self-employed / contractor.

Similarly, in a Trucking Company: If a Driver is driving your truck, he should be an employee, but if he his driving his own truck in your company, he can be a 1099-Worker.

There are several jobs those can be put in either category.

Therefore, there are two major categories of employees: one is "Employee" and the other is "Sub-Contractor". "Sub-Contractors" who are not basically your employees, I am putting them as employees because some employers tend to hire them all the time and in practical sense, they treat them as employees as for as duties are concerned but for compensation purpose they treat them contractors or sub-contractors though the practice is not permitted by IRS. But still some employers hire some of their employee as 1099-Worker, thinking IRS will not be able to figure out that rather they should be W2-Employees.

Major Tax Difference:

Employers have to put their employees on payroll, which means they should be on paid wages, salaries and compensations through the payroll system. Payroll system is a complicated process. Employees get gross salary less taxes withheld. Taxes being withheld from the employees,' wages are numerous such as Federal Income Tax, State Income Tax, Social Security Tax, Medicare Tax, Unemployment Tax, Disability Tax etc, and then employees will get the net salary. The rates of these taxes are different and I am not able to make an exact calculation. Such calculations are based on family status, family size, level of income etc. But you can say that if someone's gross salary is $100/- net may be $70/-. Not only this, every employer has to contribute some matching part towards Social Security and Medicare and Unemployment taxes, those, roughly can be calculated about 10% of gross salary.

In the case of 1099 a self-employed employee does not go through the payroll system. He will get net compensation without any deduction. It is a separate issue that such employees are subject to 15% self-employment tax up to threshold other than income tax on their personal income. At the same time employer does not contribute its matching portion of Social Security & Medicare taxes under "Federal Insurance Contribution Act (FICA). These taxes are commonly called FICA Taxes. In certain way the scheme may look beneficial to both: employees-employers at least for the time being. But such a scheme may not be desirable at IRS level. So, one has to be careful. In case of findings by IRS, an employer may be subject to heavy penalties those may also include the amount of tax evasion of employer and employee.

Other disadvantages to 1099-Worker:

- He may not be covered in Workers' Comp Insurance in case of any miss happing.
- He will be responsible for all FICA Taxes and will miss employers' matching portion to these taxes.
- He will not be covered for Unemployment Compensation during his unemployment period and Disability benefits during his disability.
- He may not participate in Group Health Plans
- He may not participate Employers' Retirement Plans

In nutshell, he will lose all those benefits, which are available to an employee due to this miss classification of his employment status.

Treating an individual as 1099-Worker instead he should be treated as W2-Employee, is a big violation for IRS stand point, unless really one is 1099-Worker.

How this violation triggers;

- During payroll audits.
- During complaint by one individual and that can trigger the audit of all 1099-workers.
- During any litigation between employer and 1099-Worker.
- During some miss happening with 1099-Worker.
- When a 1099-Worker applies for any benefit for which he is not entitled for such as unemployment benefit.
- During a complaint by 1099-Worker to Labor Department for any dispute with employer such as unpaid wages.
- During audit of either of company or individual.

Even a single case may results in opening of all other cases of miss classification.

Caution: Some employers may think that a written contract between the employer & worker may be sufficient for an employer for his legal safety. But before 20-Factor-Test, no such contract is taken to be valid.

Payroll Audits:

During payroll audits, usually the tax authorities mostly focus on several points of deficiencies:

- Single or family-owned corporation's setup to avoid the payroll taxes or where owners are getting salary less than market/billing rate.
- Considering an employee as 1099-contractor instead of W2-wage employee.

- Paying employees including owners and shareholders tax able perks as per Diem or reimbursement of business expenses or adjusting salary part as business expenses (non-taxable) and out of payroll system.
- Considering payroll items (must be paid through payroll system, such as Salary, Wages, Hourly rate, overtime, salary arrears, back salary, bonuses, variables, appreciation salary, paid vacations, salary in lieu of holidays/leave accumulations, perks & much more) as non-salary items.
- Considering taxable perks, as non-taxable perks: refer to IRS Publication 15-B for detailed study of taxable perks.
- Where employees are not paid minimum wages or paid for less hours than the actual hours worked.
- Not computing and paying for over time at over time rates.
- Not maintaining the payroll records: time sheets/punching cards, cancelled pay checks/images, copies of pay stubs, copies of payroll tax returns.
- Not paying wages in reasonable time and running a reasonable and regular payroll cycle.
- Not depositing payroll taxes and filing payroll tax returns on regular due basis.
- Running payroll without workers' comp insurance.
- Hiring and paying wages out of payroll cycle such as cash payments and hiring undocumented workers.
- Hiring underage workers without proper hiring documents-refer to the child hiring requirements.
- NJ State Labor Dept has special concern on wages those are less than the base taxable wages of unemployment and disability tax-currently it is $39,800 (2022) that increases every year.

- Not displaying payroll related several posters such as minimum wage, proof of coverage of worker com, safety policies, environments, harassment complaint system etc.
- Not maintaining employees' folders with job application, tax & immigration documents, driving license, social security card. W-4 & time sheets and all other hiring documents.
- Other related violations case to case basis.

Record Retention Requirement:

1. **Payroll Record**: Keep employment tax records for at least 4 years after the date that the tax becomes due or is paid, whichever is later.

Business Transactions: Record retain requirement is different in different situation.

- For Normally and correctly filed returned: 3 years.
- Keep records for 7 years if you file a claim for a loss from worthless securities or bad debt deduction.
- Keep records for 6 years if you do not report income that you should report, and it is more than 25% of the gross income shown on your return.
- Keep records indefinitely if you do not file a return.
- Keep records indefinitely if you file a fraudulent return.
- Some record you may have to retain for longer time, than required in normal expenses. Such as you purchased an asset and depreciating for 15 years. You should keep the record for 15 years and more of this asset.

Employment Documentations

Employer should collect the following documents from the employee upon new hiring of employees:

1. Copy of resume (Optional but desirable).

2. Employment application form (Optional but desirable). Application form you can develop your own keeping in view your business features and needs or standard format are available from the stationery stores.

3. Copy of Green Card, Work Authorization, Work Visa or any other form of Immigration document allowing the candidate to work legally in the USA. Original should be checked and copy should be kept in your record. Remember this formality is important for immigrant aliens, but not for USA born citizen.

4. Checking of references: The process is more common and desirable to check from the companies about the performance and character of the employees with previous employers.

5. Copy of Social Security Card (Original to be checked, copy to be retained).

6. Copy of Driver License (Original to be checked, copy to be retained).

7. I-9 Form. Form is prescribed by the US immigration department (Mandatory). Purpose of the form is to check the legal status of an employee. Form is filled and signed by the employer and retained by the employers. Upon any audit by labor department, the will demand of this form. *is important.*

8. W-4 (Mandatory) Form is prescribed by the IRS. Form is filled up by the employee but will be retained by employer. The purpose of the form is for withholding payroll taxes according to employees *plans* and his size of family. Upon any change in employees' situation, a new form should be collected. Once in a year, all employees should file new forms.

9. Copy of Advertisement, if any.

10. Copies of Certificates, Degree and Experience certificates

11. Employment Contract (Optional) employment contract may be necessary for certain type of business where certain commitment and serious observation is needed or where employee is going to handle right protective information and confidential work is to be assigned. For example, Computer and

Software professionals and developers' employees are given very responsible assignments.

12. Back Ground Check and Credit History Check (Optional): It is also preferred to have a back ground check of employees before hiring them. At least for responsible positions.

13. Drug Test (Optional): In these days, employers are serious about the drug testing of employees. If you are one of them, you can follow this process as well.

14. Orientation: It desirable that the company should set up a good orientation program for new employees. The program should cover various topics depending the business goals. Nature of Business, Business expectations, Company's benefits structures, company's termination policies, company's promotions and salary raises policies, timings, dress code, site visit etc. This program should be effective, because in USA employee-employer relations are crucial and subject to fast legal actions. It is better that both the parties should be aware of each other policies and expectations.

15. Implementing Programs: An employer also needs to implement various "Employment Programs" specially good for new hires and new immigrants to share basic knowledge on:

- Employees' Rights
- Employees Contractual Obligations
- Company's Goals
- Policies against sexual harassment, racial discriminations etc.
- Complaints system
- References of agencies for any complaints: Such as Labor Department, Consumer Affairs Department etc.

16. Posters Displays: An employer has to display mandatorily various kinds of posters, relating with Sexual Harassment, Complaint Procedures, Wage Policies, Discrimination etc, as designed by Federal and State Governments.

17. Employees' Handbook: A good size employers also design an Employees' Handbook containing all rules and policies of the Company and details of employees' benefit plans.

Sources of Employment

Retaining Employees

Retaining good employees is a big issue. Due high demand of employees and due to professional growth opportunities in the economy, employees are more hard to retain. First thing this country is more employees oriented than employers. It is true that finding appropriate skilled employees is a big issue, because there is always shortage of workers. There are common sources of finding the employees. USA has limited population and employment rate is high. Hunting for good employees is an on-going process for the employers. At the same time employers are also careful for hiring new employees and do not go blindly to offer the jobs.

Main sources of employment are:

Newspapers/Internet advertisements: This is most conventional method. It does not have any negative part except cost and employer itself has to do all processing and screening. Employers usually receive a large number of responses and the job of selecting the right person will become more costly and time consuming. An Employer has to sort and read all resumes, check their availability and salary requirement, check their references, immigration status, and call them for interview. US economy is a busy economy and most of employers do not have the time for all such lengthy and time-consuming processes.

Why large number of applications? People respond to advertisement in large number, that does not mean they are unemployed but for other reasons such as:

• Some are planning to switch their current employer

- Some are trying to apply for senior jobs, upper than where they are now.
- Some just came out of a new type of training.
- Some want to change the industry
- Some want to change the work
- Some are looking for higher salary
- Some are really unemployed.

It is also a tendency to change the job off and on in USA

So, in this environment finding the right person become more difficult, because most of candidates even change their resume according to an employer need, and now the employer has to be more careful.

In USA as a common practice the main important document is "Resume" of candidate, where he includes all his education, experience & achievements. There is no practice of inspecting original certificates & degrees. An employer has to depend on candidate's representation made in his resume, but he will check reference from previous employers. Reason employers want the results. If an employee could not bring the results as per expectation of the employer, he will lose the job.

Employment through Agencies:

Hiring employees through agencies are another good source of employment. The system is really good, because even employment agencies are specialized in their area of expertise. Such as agencies for accounting employees, agencies for medical practitioners, factory worker, store help, cooks, drivers, programmers and so on.

Agency system is considered efficient because they have good databases of available employees and they have tested them for job before they send the applicants to prospective employers. All references, immigration status, salary negotiations are almost completed by them beforehand.

Only negative part is that an employer has to pay them a referral fee, which could be as high as of some percentage of annual salary or at some flat rate. This referral fee is one time and some time with a guarantee of employers' satisfaction with probation period of 30-90 days.

Though the system is good, but not suitable for so many positions and for all kind of employers. Even such agencies may not have employees of your choice. So, the system is not a foolproof.

Temp-Agencies: There is another form of agencies, those provide employees for temporary positions. They function like this they will provide the employees. But you will not be paying the salary to the employees directly. You will pay to the agencies at the rate as agreed for per hour/day. Agency will keep some part of the billing for their profit and will pay the salary to the employees through their own payroll system. So, such employees are on the payroll of the agency, but they work at your spot.

Such a plan is successful for part-time employment or for short term employment, such as 4 hours a day, or 2 days a week. Practically it will be hard for you to get employee(s) on part time basis, such as 4 hours a day or 2 days a week. But an agency can, because agency will have other employers like yours, those will also need employees on a part time basis. The system is very clear, such employees will be the employees of agency and agency will keep sending its employees to different employers on par time basis as per each employer's need. Now one same employee will work for different employers through an agency and will have a full-time salary.

The other benefit that such agencies are highly specialized in their area of expertise, and their employees are fully trained. Such employees are efficient and fast, and agencies have quick replacement if an employer is not satisfied with one employee or if employee leaves the job. Such temp agencies also keep some kind of supervision on its employees through periodical reviews.

The other benefit of such agencies, that an employer need not to worry about employee benefits or employee's complaints or employees disputes.

If an employer wants to hire a Temp-employee permanently, he can do so as per contract by paying additional fee to the Agency.

Again, this system is also not foolproof. First thing, the employment is costly because employer has to pay for agency's profit. Employees have to focus on several employers at a time. So some psychology may be there that employee is not emotionally attached with the employer or may not be fully focused due to his commitment with several employers.

References: This system is really appreciated and works well for employers and employees both. Usually, when an employer has openings, it will ask its good employees to find employees from their circle. Now, existing employees will refer the candidates from their families and friends or known circle. Usually, existing employees want to remain in good books of the employer, therefore, they will try to refer the really good person known to them. Such a candidate will also be careful at employer's site, because he has been referred by a known person. But this system is also not foolproof. Existing employees may not have any known candidate for the position, or they do not want to refer for personal reasons. On the other hand, employer may also be suspicious that the company should not have a lobby of friends and families.

Anyhow, these are some common methods of hiring the employees, and one can pick up one or another suitable method.

Retaining the Employees:

Retaining employees is a serious problem. Employees are more aware about their rights, and lot of protective agencies are there to protect them, such as labor department. Country is full of attorneys specialized in protecting employees' rights. Changing employment or companies is very common. A country is full of opportunities, and employees keep enhancing their employability and keep looking for better opportunities. They keep soliciting for better Corporations having high salaries, better benefits, better promotion chances and other facilities. Companies inside job environment or personal employers' love & emotional relation between employer & employee does not work before better opportunity outside.

A business can suffer due to sudden resignation of their key employee(s).

Therefore, it becomes important for an employer to develop various policies to retain the employees as well as to maintain some kind of backup system. I will like to discuss few tips here.

- Employers should set up a salary structure related with employees' performance. If employees know that they are being paid according to their performance, he will like to stay. Such as you can decide a salary together with commission or bonus.

- Employers should setup some kind of periodical salary review system, wherein employees are to be considered for raises on the basis of periodical reviews.

- Employers should provide other motivation according to various motivational theories including, financial and non-financial.

- Employers should provide a competitive package of benefits of similar businesses or better.

Backup Support.

A Company should also keep a backup support for key functions employees. For example, in case of Diner/Restaurant Business, if key Cook quits the job, diner will not be able to run. For other businesses key employee may be somebody else.

Termination of Employees:

Termination of employees is a common practice in USA that is commonly known as Firing from job. "I got fired" is a common slang, the terminated employees will use. Getting fired is not considered most of the something insulted or barrier for reemployment though it causes financial hardships for short time. And terminations will not be a serious negative factor for another employment, unless of serious violation or fraud.

Employees are fired for the main following reasons:

- Poor Financial Position of the employer.
- Reduction in Sale.
- Under a Cost cut programs and plans.
- Mergers
- Poor performance of employee
- Misunderstanding with management
- Under disciplinary action
- Some other special reason.

But a good company should keep a record of reasons for firing, because a wrongful termination can create legal hassles for employer. More over employee can ask the reason of his termination.

I will give you few examples. If you are terminating due to reduction in your sale or revenue, you should keep the record of such reductions.

If you are terminating for disciplinary actions, you should write down for your record for such violations, and keep records of warnings given. If someone is in the habit of coming late, you should write down the dates and times and some sort of history of warnings given on this account.

It will be much better if you formally design set of" Termination Policy" of the Company. Again, for example, some franchised may have termination policies for their cashier employees that if cash is found shorter more than $10 three times during 3 months, five times more then $5/-, a cashier employee can be terminated. A cashier whose cash is found short more then $20/- can be fired same days such as. Even some companies may have policy that employee can be fired being late for 5 minutes. I heard a story that even a corporate officer was fired for using the company's postal stamp. USA is a disciplined country so you can make termination policies based on strict discipline with a room for exceptions.

Even some employers are using the practice of getting signed of pre "employment contract". Such a contract itself should define the terms and conditions of employment. Keep in mind that such contract should not over and above the American laws and Federal and State Constitutions. As an employer you may not be able to put terms and conditions contrary to the American Laws. An Employment Contract should not tend to even slight slavery or jeopardize fundamental rights. It is better to get such contracts drafted by the attorney or you should take the advice of a legal expert or an attorney.

Some Employers use to write terms and conditions in the job offer letter, and such letters are duly signed by the employees as "accepted", and a copy is returned to the employer.

But most of the jobs are based on verbal understanding.

Wage Policies:

There are two types of wage policies:

1) Salary Based Employees

2) Hourly Based Employees

1) Salary based Employees: These are senior level employees who get a fixed salary for a year. Their salary check is amounted for the amount of annual salary divided by total annual pay periods. Such employees or officers or manager works during normal business hours. And may have to sit late or come early with or without additional compensation, dependent on business practice. Their compensation is not related with strictly number of hours worked, rather they are at higher level and will be working for the business at additional and flexible times as well. Most of such position may involve an employment contract.

2) Hourly Based Employees

Such employees are paid for the number of hours they work. They are paid wages for the number of hours worked times the wage rate during a pay period. For such employees', employers have to follow strict wage policies:

Maintaining of Time Card: Employers have to introduce some sort of system for keeping the time record of each employee. When they start the work, when they go for lunch, when they leave the work etc. This provision is good to keep track of employee's inputted time, to generate the salary and is the requirement of labor department. In these days, there are lots of systems to maintain employees time records. Most common system is card punching machines, those are economical, easy to use, and most popular. Each employee has his own card in the shelf. They will punch the card in the punching machine, at the time of arrival and departures. Punching machine will punch the time of arrival and departure and will calculate the hours (time inputted). Some employers have computerized system of time tracking where employees use their unique id number for start and end times.

Number of Hours: No employee should be asked to work more than 40 hours a week during 5 days week. If someone works more than 40 hours, as per the job requirement, employers have to pay the overtime at a higher rate of wage that is one and a half times of regular wage rate.

Over Time Salary: For example suppose an employee's hourly rate is \$20/hour, and he works 60 hours in a week. (Calculation will need on weekly basis). He must be paid = 40x20+**20x30**=\$1400.

But it is not necessary that one should work a maximum of 8 hours a day. I heard some employees enjoy flexibility, especially in health industry, to complete 40 hours in 4 days or even less if they want. Rest of the week they can enjoy holidays or can work for over time if employer wants so. But this option is not in the hands of employees, but in the hands of those of such employers.

Minimum Wage: Employers have to give each employee minimum wage rate specified by the Federal/State Governments. Each State has its own minimum wage rate. Average minimum wage rate is \$15.00 per hour. But remember in these days employees may ask for higher rates.

Pay Period: Employers can pay salary on monthly basis, semimonthly, bi-weekly (two weeks) or on weekly basis.

But for hourly rate employees, employees should get salary on weekly basis or bi-weekly basis. The most common practice is weekly basis for hourly rate employees. Employers can also have different pay periods for different employees or employees' group or employees' categories. So, in a year the total pay period could be:

Monthly Basis	12
Semi-monthly	24
Bi-weekly	26
Weekly	52

Pay Day:

Usually, employers fixed the pay day as per Labor Department's guidelines. It is really hard to pay the salary or wages during the same week for the same week. But still there is good number of employers those who pay the salary on each Friday. Friday eve is a special happy evening for employees. Lets have few examples:

Pay Day every Wednesday: Will cover the salary of previous week(s).

(Monday to Sunday)

Payday every Friday: Will cover the salary of previous week(s).

Every 10th of month: Will cover the salary of previous month.

(1st to Last Date of Month)

Pay Day Wednesday is usually good for bi-weekly salary because employees are financially tight in two weeks cycle, so they should be paid at the earliest possible.

Thursday: Some employers have chosen Thursday for different reasons also. For them, Wednesday is too early to process the paychecks, and Thursday is better. Thursday is not a Friday; the day people spend all the money on fun. So, Thursday they may not spent the money rather may take home for homely needs.

Friday: Employers can pay on Friday, that will make employees' Friday eve more special though they save the money for home or not.

Fair Wage

In some type entity owner/shareholder will have to be on payroll especially in revenue generating entity such as Corporation/S-Corporation.

Fair Wage means what should be salary of an active owners or shareholders of Corporation or S Corporation and or LLC.

Wage concept for LLC members does not exist, but instead Guaranteed Payments to active partners/members can be arranged, those who are considered providing extra services in business, but that too is not mandatory. Such decision are done through Partnership Operating Agreements.

In case of S Corporation/C Corporation the active owners (shareholders), should get salary and should be on payroll. Next question, how much should be the salary? Answer: Fair wage!

S Corporation status entities manage total distribution of profit, part as a salary and part as a profit. Because distribution of profit is not subject to payroll taxes (15.3% Employee/Employer), and therefore, salary is strategic in way to reduce the overall tax obligation. For example, getting distribution less in salary and more in profit, though reasonable wage rule always exited.

Here is logical discussion what should be a reasonable salary of an active owner/shareholder in compliance.

1) Market Rate: What he will get, if he works for someone else: based on his experience and credentials in identical businesses.
2) Counter Part Rate (Comparison): What his counterparts are getting in same kind of industry and skill.
3) What was his salary immediate before starting his own S Corporation in same line of service?
4) Owner's responsibility, time, skill level in his own Corporation compare to other employees in his own Corporation. Example: A full active Lawyer should not get less salary than his juniors.

5) Owner's billing rate: where owner works for Corporation's clients, and charges for his services. Example: IT Consultant: His wage, benefits, payroll taxes should be enough close to his productivity.

6) Sole owner and Sole earner: Example: IT Consultant, CPA, Attorney etc. His salary plus benefits should be equal to net profit. All distributions are wages.

These logics are more valid in-service businesses, where revenue is generated by personal services of the owners. But in other businesses the logic may not be so good because revenues are generated based on other factors such as investment, inventory, assets & goodwill.

The above logics are valid only depending on "condition of business".

Examples:

1) An employee working for $100,000 started his own S Corporation. In the First few years, it generated revenue of $5,000-$10,000, so his previous salary, market rate, skill and experience, concept is not valid here.

2) A CPA works in his own Corporation in Woodbridge NJ, another works in Manhattan, so the comparison concept is not valid here.

3) A CPA Partner works on audit assignments, and other works on tax preparation, so comparison concept in own Corporation is not valid, rather this is will based on employee performance.

In summary reasonable compensation should be based:

1) Employee Performance
2) Employee Productivity
3) Salary Comparisons and
4) Company Condition.
5) Employee's Participation Level

Guaranteed Payments: In LLC-Partnership. Salary concept is not available in Partnership, but alternatively Guaranteed Payments can be arranged for active partners. This is a compensating arrangement that does not impact the total tax liability, because Guaranteed Payments and the Share of profit, for an active partners or members , both are subject to self-employment tax.

However, the major diversions will depend on case-to-case basis, and may need justifiable circumstances in various unforeseen business conditions.

Advertisement & Marketing of Business

Advertisement is another component of making your business a success. If you do not believe in advertisement, you may have to advertise to sell your business. Advertisement has become something really important for your business to be a successful venture. But you have to be careful to pick up the mode of advertisement. There are lots of modes of advertisements with lots of agencies, magazines, newspapers, radios, tv etc. But some time it is really hard to find the most effective way and most effective mode of advertisement. Advertisements are good in modes for different agencies for different types of businesses. The sales persons working for different agencies and newspapers may try to make you confused, but you are the only person who can find the proper advertisement mode. Also keep in mind that the advertisements are very costly, plus there may not be immediate output. I heard from several business people that even some advertisements are not so effective to cover the cost of advertisement itself.

Some of the Advertising Modes:

Newspaper Advertisements:

Newspapers Advertisements are the most common mode of advertisements. They differ in the matter of types of newspapers.

Their effectiveness will also depend on the newspapers, circulation area, ethnic group involved etc.

Types of Newspapers:

- Daily Newspapers
- Weekly Newspapers
- Free Newspapers
- Subscribed Newspapers.
- American Newspapers
- Newspapers of different ethnic groups: Such as Indian Newspapers, Chines Newspapers etc.

Types of Newspaper Advertisements:

Displayed Advertisements: Such ads are very costly and are inserted and designed by using graphics and banners etc. Such advertisements are available in different ranges and also in different locations in a newspapers. Their prices go with the size and location in the newspapers but are considered comparatively more effective and show a big business setup.

Classified Advertisements: These are less expensive but inserted without graphics.

Their prices and locations are almost standardized in the newspapers.

Business Directory Advertisements: Some Newspapers have special section in their newspapers calling Business or Service Directory. This section provides some sort of listing in advertisement shape of businesses in category type. The location and prices are also utmost standard.

It is some time hard to choose that which Newspapers and which type of advertisement will be more effective and should also meet your budget.

Service providing businesses usually believe that Listing in Business Directory in 'free newspapers' is good for results and also available cheap in affordable prices.

On the other hand, to show yourself a big *rich* and successful business, and to attract the attention of readers' you may have to depend on graphic advertisements.

TV Ads:

Another media for advertising your business is through TV ads. TV ads are considered more effective though they are very costly. The consecutive repetition of advertisement, business people say really works.

There are several TV companies and channels. Some channels are regional and of in your country language. In USA there are at least 3 –5 Indian channels. Same way there are channels for other countries. Again, choosing a channel for your business advertisement is very technical jobs. Perhaps you may need professional consulting.

Radio Ads:

Like TV ads, radio ads are costly also. Same way we have different radio frequencies, some are for different languages and presenting programs in different countries languages. I know two good stations those are specifically run in Indian languages. Their musical programs are in Hindi and they broadcast Hindi songs twenty-four hours of the day. Most Indian business people are choosing these stations for advertising their businesses.

Mailing: Another mode of advertising your business is mass mailing. The problem in massing mailing is obtaining or gathering the database. Mailing is really costly and time-consuming mode.

Sources of Data: There are several agencies, which sells databases via CD/Software. You can also generate your own database for local customers using phone books or business listings available on Internet.

There are several mass mailing agencies. They will mail your flyers along with other businesses' flyers or letters.

There are virtually several advertisements modes that may include distribution of flyers, billboard signs, issuing discount coupons, sales coupon, seminars, joining associations etc. depending on the type of business. But in USA the word of mouth (referral) is considered the most effective mode of advertisement that means people tell others about your business. So, one may have to depend on several modes of advertisements.

Web Site Developing: In these days developing your business Web Site is common, and taken a good source of marketing.

Marketing through social media: There are about 40 social media apps, the most common are:

- Snapchat
- LinkedIn
- YouTube
- TikTok
- WhatsApp
- Instagram
- Reddit
- Facebook
- Twitter
- Telegram

Each type of app is easy to use and can be used for different modes of marketing.

Customers Service: Concept of Customer service is very strong in USA. As we discussed that business in USA is highly competitive.

Everyone can think to compete on price. But there *are* is certain level from there you cannot go more down, while others may, because other may have lower overheads or may be working on volume. The next thing would be quality. If you are limited with these two factors, then the next would-be customers' service. Customers' service includes the concept that you consider "Customer is Always Right". You are supposed to believe all the complaints true and worth consideration. You will be agreeing to the customers' argument up to customers' satisfaction. You will be appreciating customers' liking or not liking or his tastes. You will help them to pick up the item the way they want. You will meet them with greetings whether they do any business with you or not. You will take all their negative remarks regarding the products in a normal and friendly way. Even if they purchase some product, and later do not like it and want to return, you will take it back without any serious question or restriction.

At the same time, you may have your reservation on price, warranty, final sale or representing your point of view in way that customers' should be able to realize your logic or point really relevant to it.

Taxes

USA taxation system is immense and real complex. The total discussion is out of scope. But I will give you some introduction on several types of taxes. One can group all these taxes into following categories:

Personal Tax
Business Tax
Payroll Tax
Sales Tax
Other Taxes

Personal Tax: Out of scope of this manual.

Some Important Tax Forms for businesses:

All Types of Businesses have to file annual income Tax Returns with Federal and States of their Registrations.

Sole Proprietors (including self-employed and 1099-NEC Worker)

IRS Form: 1040: US Individual Income Return: Sch C: Profit and Loss from Business.

Corporations:

IRS Form: 1120-US Corporation Income Tax Return

"S" Corporations:

IRS Form:1120-S- US Income Tax Return for an S Corporation

LLCs & Partnerships

IRS Form: 1065- US Return of Partnership Income

Payroll Returns & Documents:

IRS Form 941-Employer Quarterly Tax Return: Each Quarter

IRS Tax Document: W2-Wage and Tax Statement: Annually

IRS Tax Document: 1099-NEC-Non-Employment Compensation-Annually

Normal Tax Filings Due Last Dates: For Calendar Year Filers.

- 1120S-S Corp-IRS: March 15th- NJ April 15th.
- CBT 100-S : S Corp NJ: April 15th (IRS has March 15th.)
- LLC: Multi Members (2 & +): For IRS : March 15th. : For NJ: April 15th.
- Single Member LLC (Sch C Filer): April 15th for IRS/NJ.

- Single Member &/or multi members LLC opted to file S Corp: March 15th for NJ: April 15th.
- C Corp-1120 IRS/NJ: April 15th.
- Single Member &/or multi members LLC opted for C Corp-1120: April 15th.
- 1040 Series Individuals: Self Employer, Sole proprietors : Sch C April 15th.
- Last date for claiming refund: three years limit: April 15th
- Filing FBAR: Form 114: April 15th.

PS: Usual deadlines of March 15th and April 15th are extended to cover for certain Holidays, Saturdays, and Sundays.

Business Accounting

Items of Accounting for Business Taxes:

Different entities are taxed differently. Anyhow I will discuss each profit entity in the following paragraphs. But one common thing to all businesses is "business accounting".

Businesses are taxed on net income, and method of arriving at net income is almost same for each type of business. For example; net profit is arrived after deducting all business expenses almost in all types of business.

You have to prepare your financial Statements according to the format of accounting standard of USA. Basic elements are:

Categories of business revenues

Categories of business expenses

Total Revenue less cost of goods sold = Gross profit

Gross Profit less Operating expenses = Gross Net Profit

Net profit-Depreciation etc = Net Taxable Profit (*Taxable)*

What kind of Revenue is to be included in "Revenue"? You will include all the receipt on account of sale or service into the total of revenue. Other categories of revenue could be rebates, discounts, bank interest, refunds of prior expenses, commissions and or other miscellaneous income. But you can deduct all amounts refunded to customer or good returned by the customers or any such allowance for credit given to customers as sales returns.

Expenses: From your total revenue you can deduct your business expenses such as:

Cost of goods sold (if applicable)
Advertisement
Compensation
Salary & Wages
Rent
Business Traveling
Office Supplies
Telephone
Repair
Utilities
Employees Benefit Programs
Licensing
Franchise Fee
Management Fee
And so on.......

There is no limit or specified percentage. Only limit is that all business expenses should be reasonable and necessary to conduct the business and should be restricted only to business activities.

IRS also wants you to keep proof of all business expenses supported by relevant documents such as invoices, payment receipts, business purpose, and cancelled checks. IRS frequently audits the businesses on random basis and under selective basis as special assignments, if they find your account has any over lapping in expenses or incomes.

Though there is no limit on business expenses, but IRS has issued several publications to determine the validity and eligibility of each type of business expenses and has fixed the strict eligibility criteria and limits. Each type of business expense must meet IRS guidelines in their publications to be qualified as a business deduction.

Taxation for Sole Proprietorship:

As I discussed earlier taxation for sole proprietorship is pretty easy as compare to other entities. There are two groups of Tax Returns:

Personal Tax Return

Business Tax Return

Personal Tax return is filed by the individual inserting all his income from wages, bank interest, capital gain, retirement, rental or residual income, and social security benefits. Business income etc. Personal tax return can be prepared for individual or joint including spouse income from all such sources. Usually married couples file a joint return for better tax rates and availing several credits. To treat and include income from several sources one has to prepare and attached several schedules prescribed for each type of source of income.

A Sole-proprietor will report his business income and business expenses on his personal tax return as computed by using Schedule "C". (IRS form for Profit & Loss to be filled up and attached with personal tax return). 1099-Workers & Contractors also come in this category.

Schedule "C" is an IRS schedule which asks for total receipts and total expenses in different categories to arrive at net profit. This net profit figure will move to the main tax form and will be added up with other incomes. After several adjustments on account of

Standard Deduction, Education Credit, Personal exemptions, retirement fund contributions, Child Credit, Low Income Children earned income credits etc. you will arrive at your net taxable income. So, this net taxable income that will include sole proprietorship income as well, will be taxed as per tax brackets and tax rates, which mean high income will be taxed at a higher rate.

Sole proprietorship income is also subject to self-employment tax @ 15.3% as calculated on Schedule "C".

Therefore, sole proprietorship net income becomes subject to two types of taxes. One is income tax (if after all adjustments still it is a taxable income) other is self-employment tax.

A Taxpayer's income may or may not be subject to income tax, because there are several adjustments available, but self-employment tax is straight forward on net business income.

What is Self-employment Tax: Do not consider self-employment tax as an additional burden. The purpose of self-employment tax is to generate old age benefits for you. The Government thinks that an employee can generate old age benefits through payroll tax deduction. Same way a sole proprietor who is not an employee anywhere, should also generate at same pattern old age benefit that include social security and medicate benefits through self-employment tax. Self-employment tax is a sort of substitute of payroll tax for contractor and self-employed workers.

Corporation Tax:

As discussed earlier that, there are two types of Corporations, "C" type of Corporation and "S" type of Corporation. So, each type of Corporation is taxed differently.

"C" Type of Corporation: C type of Corporation is also known as regular Corporation. This type of Corporation is subjected to double taxation, which means, whatever is net profit of the Corporation, a Corporation will pay tax on that figure. Tax will be computed by using tax rates prescribed for Corporation. After computing tax on its net profit, whatever is left, a Corporation may have two options. First, they can keep the money with Corporation:

1.   As retain earning for future use: But this is not source of savings rather there should be purpose behind it such to pay backs loans, future expansion plans etc.

2.   Use the Money for Investment or Expansion

3.   Distribute among Shareholders as dividend

As per the Corporation's policies. If they distribute the money to shareholders as a "Dividend" and then that amount will be included in the personal tax return of each shareholder, and thus each shareholder will pay the tax on such distributed "Dividends" as per his tax rates and tax brackets.

"S" Corporation Taxation: An "S" Corporation is not a taxable entity as discussed earlier. The net income so arrived will be apportioned to all its shareholders in the ratio of their shares' (ownership) percentage. Such allocated apportioned amount of profit or loss will be included in the personal tax return of each shareholder under income item define for "S" Corporation income, and it will become the part of other source income and will be taxed according to the tax rates and tax brackets.

There is a key difference between a "C" Corporation and an "S" Corporation's net profit. In the case of "C" Corporation a shareholder will be taxed only if he receives the dividend (part of net profit as dividend), but in "S" Corporation a shareholder will be taxed on the allocated share of net profit whether he receives the money or not. But if a shareholder does not receive the full amount of the allocated share of net profit, the balance will increase his amount of equity in the business. Other important issue is that allocated share of net income is not subject to "self-employment tax".

LLC (Limited Liability Companies) Taxation: As discussed, LLC is more or less a flexible entity. For tax purposes, its members can choose whether it to be taxed as a Partnership or as a Corporation. Similarly, a single member LLC can elect to be taxed as a sole proprietorship or as a Corporation. Therefore, an LLC will be taxed the way it elects to be taxed.

Partnership: A Partnership is also not a taxable entity. But it has to file its own tax return that includes detailed items of income and expenses and net profit. The net profit or loss so arrived will be allocated to each partner in the decided percentage of interest in LLC. Again, these figures will be included in their personal tax returns under item specified for partnership income, and they will be taxed at the individual rates and brackets on their taxable income. Another important thing is that partnership income is also subject to self-employment tax at a rate of 15.3% for active members or partners.

Pass through Entities

Pass through entities mean that an entity does not pay income tax on its net taxable income. But net taxable income will be apportioned to its owners/ partners/ members /shareholders in their respective ratios, and they will include their apportioned share in their personal income tax returns, and will pay income tax at their personal tax brackets.

- Partnership
- LLC (including other types of such entities)
- S Corporation.

All these are called "Pass through Entities".

Hard facts about Pass through Entities: Pass through Entities: Allocate the net profit to their members or shareholders, whether equal cash has been paid or not.

For example: Such an entity has allocated certain amount to its members or shareholders. But instead paying cash to them, had invested in expansion. Members will pay tax on allocated amount whether they receive cash or not. But so unpaid share of their profit will increase their equity, and in future they can take cash without tax, because they have already paid the tax on this previous apportioned amount of profit.

How much a business has to pay in taxes: This is common question every new prospective business wants to know. But answer is not that simple. Even answer to roughly amount of tax not so simple. It involves a complex tax computations and tax accounting. Each item of revenue and each item of expense has to be treated under IRS guidelines and limits. There may be several credits and incentives or there may be several expenses those are not fully deductible. Once these all computations are completed and tax will be calculated according to the tax rates and tax table depending on taxable entity or individual taxpayer on net taxable amount. Every year IRS and State Tax agencies come up with several changes and modification in tax policies and issues tax rates for different entities and filing status those are easily available in local libraries and on Internet.

Payroll Taxes

Introduction to Payroll Taxes

This has always been an issue with all types of employees and for some employers to understand the payroll taxes. The detail and complex discussion will be out of scope from this book but I can provide a basic introduction to payroll taxes.

People always come up with the question how much percentage goes into payroll taxes?? There is no straightforward percentage rather it is a combination of several types of taxes, and each type has its own rate and base amount. Similarly, each type of tax has its own coverage and relation to a certain benefit program.

Why we have so many payroll Taxes?? Because all these deductions go to different benefit programs as defined by Federal and State Governments.

People come up with the question that I have so much deduction from paycheck and why I am not getting refund?? Because your all payroll deductions are not of income tax deductions rather meant for different benefit programs defined by Federal and State. You will be benefited from these programs in future and on being qualified and eligible.

Some people are upset about so much money and so many payroll Taxes. But there should be no reason, as you see the benefits attached to such deductions. The whole system is for our welfare and financial help during old age, sickness, disability and unemployment.

Would these benefits be enough for an individual?? No. such benefits may be limited and may not be sufficient to meet individual needs. Most of these benefits will depend on the length of services and your total gross taxable salary. Therefore, people may have to plan well ahead of time to participate in other private and additional plans.

But it is important for employers to understand payroll taxes for their own tax planning, cost of hiring, fiduciary obligation and answers to their employees for payroll tax questions.

List of Payroll Taxes:

There is a list of taxes that are systematically withheld (deducted) from the salary of an employee by the employer and are remitted to related Federal and State Tax agencies. The payroll deduction process is well defined by the IRS and State where employer have almost no choice. Regarding payroll taxes employer is a trustee and does fiduciary duties between the employee and tax agencies.

In addition to an employee's salary/wage deductions for different taxes, an employer has to contribute as his match share towards certain payroll taxes. Employers' payroll taxes are also well defined and are to be contributed systematically as per prescribed rates and tax bases.

We would like to provide you the list of such taxes by using New Jersey State and year 2022.

EMPLOYEE				EMPLOYER	
Sl.#	DESCRIPTION	RATE	BASE AMOUNT In $	RATE	BASE AMOUNT In $
1.	Social Security Tax	6.2%	147,000	6.2%	147,000
2.	Medicare Tax	1.45%	No Limit	1.45%	No Limit
3.	Federal Unemployment	0	N/A	0.8%	7,000.00
4.*	Federal Income Tax Withholding	As per Tax Brackets and Tax Tables	No Limit	N/A	N/A
5.*	State Income Tax Withholding	As per Tax Brackets and Tax Tables	No Limit	N/A	N/A
6.**	NJ Unemployment Insurance	0.3825%	39,800	2.4825%	39.800
7.	NJ Health Care Subsidy	0.00	N/A	0.2%	39,800
8.	NJ Workforce Development	.0425%	24,900.	.1175%	39,800
9.	NJ Disability Insurance	0.5%	39,800	0.5%	39,800

*Base Amount is subject to change every year to cover the inflation.

**Income Tax is withheld according to tax brackets and tax tables set by IRS and State Tax Agencies. The amount of withholding will depend on several factors, such as:

Amount of Gross Salary

Marriage Status

Number of Dependents

If both husband- wife are working

If eligible for any child credits

Or if the taxpayer needs additional tax withholding.

Income tax is a tax on income, income from all sources including salary and it is only employees' responsibility. Employer is more concerned about deduction of income tax from salary as per information provided by the employee by using form W-4. Final Tax liability will be the employee's own responsibility at the yearend when he/she will prepare and file his/her personal tax return. As a computation of yearend tax liability, an employee may receive a refund on account of over withholding or may have to pay additional tax amount on account less withholding. IRS/State assesses additional amount on account of interest and penalties on less withholding if such shortage is out of defined limits.

**State Tax Rates are defined by the State for each entity by using its own experience rates. We are using just a basic example.

Sample Examples:

Let's consider one typical example:

	In $
Annual Salary	120,000.00

Monthly Salary	10,000	120,000/12
Married Status:	Married	
Total Exemptions:	3	

One for Taxpayers, One Spouse, One for Child (Family of 3 members and spouse is not working)

Pay Cycle	**Monthly**	
Monthly Gross Salary	10,000	
Deductions		
Social Security Tax	620.00	@6.2%
Medicare Tax	145.00	@ 1.45%
Federal Income Tax Withholding	1,700.00	Tax Tables:
Estimate		
NJ Income Tax Withholding	500.00	Tax Tables- Estimate
NJ unemployment Insurance	38.25	@0.3825%
NJ Health Care Subsidy	0.00	NJ
Workforce Development	4.25	@0.0.0425%
NJ Disability Insurance	50.00	@0.5%
Total Withholding/Deductions	3057.50	
Net Salary	6942.50	
Employer's Payroll Taxes		
Federal Unemployment	56.00	@0.8% of 7000.00
Social Security Tax	620.00	@ 6.2%
Medicare Tax	145.00	@ 1.45%
NJ Unemployment Tax	258.59	@ 2.4825%
NJ Healthcare Subsidy	20.83	@ 0.2%
NJ Workforce Development	12.24	@ 0.1175%
NJ Disability Insurance	52.08	@ 0.5%
Total Employer's Taxes	1164.74	

The Employee's and Employer's tax liability will be at an end, on salary beyond tax basis for certain taxes.

Let's presume that the employee's job position stays with the same employer for whole full year (Jan 01-Dec 31). In such a case the situation with payroll taxes at the year-end should be as follow: -

Illustration: Tax Rates for 2021.

Annual Gross Salary	120,000.00
7,440	Base Amount 142,800
	1,740 No Limit
15,000	No Limit: Tax Estimate
5,000	No Limit Tax Estimate
NJ Unemployment Insurance @ 0.3825%	135.03 Base Amount 35,300
0.00	
NJ Workforce Development @ .0425%	15.00 Base Amount 35,300
175.50	Base Amount 35,300
Total Deductions	**29506.54**
Total Net	**90,493.46**

Employer's Payroll Tax Liability:

Federal Unemployment Tax @ 0.8%	56.00	Base Amount 7000.00
Social Security Tax @ 6.2%	7440	Base Amount 142,800
Medicare Tax @ 1.45%	1740	No Limit
NJ Unemployment Insurance @ 2.4825%	876.33	Base Amount 35,300
NJ Healthcare Subsidy @ .2%	70.60	Base Amount 24900.00
NJ Workforce Development @ 0.1175%	41.28	Base Amount 35,300
NJ Disability @0.5%	176.50	Base Amount 24900.00
Total	**10,400.91**	

Total employment cost of an employee hiring at salary of $120,000/Yr. (10000/month) will be = 120,000+ 10,400.91=130400.91+ cost of employees' benefit programs.

It can be seen that payroll tax is not a single flat rate, but a combination of several components, with different rates and different tax base amount (thresholds)

Special feature in Payroll Taxes: Special feature in payroll tax, in some taxes if employee is responsible, and at same time employer has to contribute his matching share towards employee taxes, see in above illustrations.

Why so many payroll taxes:

This is common question asked by new hiring employees, and also by employees. Actually, all are not taxes. Most are kind of insurance premium towards several benefits on the line to an employee as he/she moves on. Such as old age retirement benefit mostly called Social Security Benefit, Medical care after age 65, Unemployment monthly benefit in case of someone loose the job, and disability benefit (full/partial) in case of accident, and so on.

Payroll Tax Reminting & Report Filing.

The employers' will be sole responsible for reminting deducted tax and filing payroll tax returns. An employer works as trustee of IRS and State governments to deducted the payroll taxes from employees' salaries, and hold the money for further remittance to all related agencies as per dead lines fixed by tax authorities.

EXAMPLE:

Suppose monthly salary:	**$10,000**
Tax Deduction:	

Social Security Tax	620.00
Medicare Tax	145.00
Federal Income Tax Withholding	1,700.00

NJ Income Tax Withholding	500.00
NJ unemployment Insurance	38.25
NJ Health Care Subsidy	0.00
NJ Workforce Development	4.25
NJ Disability Insurance	50.00
Total Withholding/Deductions	**3057.50**
Employer's Payroll Taxes	
Federal Unemployment	56.00
Social Security Tax	620.00
Medicare Tax	145.00
NJ Unemployment Tax	258.59
NJ Healthcare Subsidy	20.83
NJ Workforce Development	12.24
NJ Disability Insurance	52.08
Total Employer's Taxes	**1164.74**

As fiduciary responsibility, an employer will remit the following taxes to tax agencies in one shot on or before the due date:

IRS: Total Employee's Deductions: $ 2465+Employe'r Contribution: $821=$3286.

NJ State: Total Employee's Deductions: $592.50+ Employer's Contribution: 343.74=$936.24.

Tax Remittance Dates:

Remittance dates differ employer to employer. Actually, it will depend on the amount of total tax liability.

Monthly Depositors: By 15th of next month.

Same Day Depositors   Within 3 days of pay-checks.

Quarterly Depositors   15th of month following the quarter.

Modes of Payroll Tax Deposits:

IRS: IRS Portal-EFTPS-Electronic Federal Tax Payment System

New Jersey : Portal DORES -Division of Revenue & Enterprise Services.

Payroll Tax Returns:

Tax Filing Report Number	Filing Cycle	Deadline Date
IRS 941- Employer's Quarterly Federal Tax Return.	Quarterly	Due by the last day of the month following the end of the quarter.
IRS 940- Employer's Annual Federal Unemployment (FUTA) Tax Return.	Annually	January 31.
IRS W-3: Transmittal of Wage and Tax Statements	Annually	January 31st.
IRS W-2- Wage and Tax Statement:	Annually	January 31st.
Contractors		
IRS: 1096- Annual Summary and Transmittal of Department of the Treasury U.S. Information Returns	Annually	January 31st.
IRS 1099-NEC: Nonemployee Compensation	Annually	January 31st.
New Jersey Tax Reports		
NJ-927: State of New Jersey Employer's Quarterly Report	Quarterly	Due by the last day of the month following the end of the quarter.
WR-30 : "Employer Report of Wages Paid	Quarterly	Due by the last day of the month

		following the end of the quarter along with NJ-927.
NJ -W-3: NEW JERSEY - DIVISION OF TAXATION GROSS INCOME TAX RECONCILIATION OF TAX WITHHELD	Quarterly	January 31st.

Sales Tax & Use Tax:

Sales Tax is on all purchases (items) subject to sales which you pay at the time of buying from the retail stores or vendors , if you are the consumer or ultimate user. If you buy from a wholesaler to further resell to retailers, you are not subject to sales tax provided you have obtained the exempt certificate from your State to make such purposes. Sales tax is State tax having different rates in different States. As a business or retailer all sales taxes collected from customers, you have to remit to State according to their guidelines and have to file monthly/quarterly tax returns. Like payroll taxes, a retailer is a trustee of sales tax collected amount, and he has to remit further to the tax agencies under his fiduciary duties.

For any negligence in remitting fiduciary taxes with the tax agency, is taken serious, and the owner can be held personally for the recovery of such taxes.

Use Tax: Use tax is a part of sales tax. This mean if you as a consumer (business or individual) buy any item(s) without paying sale tax, you have to pay sales tax in your State at the rate of your State. Individuals report such purchases in their personal State tax return and business file annual reports for such purchases. Use-Tax usually arise when you buy stuff as a consumer from other States through internet and the sellers do not charge any sales tax because you live in other States that of seller's State. But if such purchase is taxable item in your State of residence, you or your business will be liable for this tax to your State.

Other Taxes: There may be several other taxes & fees Federal/States depending type of business and business location.

Which is a good business to do in USA.

Most of people as this question. But this question is not valid and hence is out of scope of this book. A kind of business is your choice. Practically all businesses are good in one or other respect. This is the reason we have all types of businesses in the economy. All businesses are though good, but all have common factor is of inherit of business risk. Therefore, you have to see, which business is good for you. There are some common factors in selecting a business:

- Prior Experience in the line of business
- Availability of funds for Investment
- Location of business
- Technology involved in business
- Availability of borrowed funds
- Availability of family and friends' support
- Availability of partners or associates
- Availability of experienced employees.
- Personal liking & excitement.

Conclusion:

This book is written by the author based on his knowledge and experience for several issues relating to a new business set up in USA, but it does not contain exclusive all. Rules & regulations in USA are so immense, complex, hidden and widely spread, cannot be covered in one book. The total exposure is out of scope of this book. Book is mostly written in layman type discussion, but author thinks, it will give a valuable knowledge to business setup seekers in the USA, and the discussion therein will work as an alerting tool in several areas if not all.

But still suggest to consult all related professionals, and material in this book should not be taken as substitute of professional advice in your situation, and so author will not take any responsibility for any information contained in this book. Therefore, it is being suggested to consult appropriate professional or agency to get accurate and Up-To-Date information.

———————

Ingram Content Group UK Ltd.
Milton Keynes UK
UKHW040751210723
425555UK00001B/49